DAVID SOLOMONS

VIKING

VIKING
An imprint of Penguin Random House LLC
375 Hudson Street
New York, New York 10014

First published in the United Kingdom by Nosy Crow, 2016
Published simultaneously in the United States of America by Viking, an imprint of Penguin
Random House LLC, 2016

LIBRARY OF CONGRESS CATALOGING-IN-PUBLICATION DATA IS AVAILABLE
ISBN 9780451474940

Printed in the USA

10   9   8   7   6   5   4   3   2   1

FOR LUKE AND LARA, the nicest invaders you could ever hope to be conquered by. We couldn't be happier that you've taken over our world, but if you wouldn't mind delaying the daily invasion until after 7 a.m., that'd be much appreciated.

POWER-UP

"Luke, use your force field," Serge shouted from the other side of the splintering ten-story shark tank that ran the height of Commander Octolux's vast undersea lair. There was a crack like a pistol shot as the tank sprang a leak, and a stream of water arced onto the deck, splashing my foot.

We were about to be up to our necks in hammerheads.

I focused my force field superpower on the widening hole. Glowing blue energy shot from my fingers and plugged the gap. That would keep the sharks at bay. Now it was Octolux's turn. I checked my watch—we had less than five minutes before he launched an intercontinental ballistic missile containing a unique and deadly payload. If we failed to stop him, then the virus stored in the warhead would infect the whole world, turning every man, woman, and child into a quivering jellyfish.

"I'm going for the command bridge," I said, sweeping

past Serge. I touched a finger to the side of my mask and with a swift tap blasted a fizzing ball of mental energy at the high-security door. It flew off its hinges and hit the floor with a clang. Quickly, I stepped over it, my cape fanning out behind me as I raced inside.

The walls of the command bridge were one smooth curve of plexiglass, offering a 360-degree view of the deep ocean. Monstrous shadows cast by dimly glimpsed sea creatures glided over the surface. The ping of the sonar and the gurgle of Octolux's breathing apparatus were the only sounds. After battling our way past attack squids, lethal lionfish sentries, and electric eel assassins, we had reached our final goal.

Commander Octolux stood over the launch control panel, preparing to fire his fishy missile. At one time he had been wholly human, but where his head used to be was now a surgically attached octopus plugged directly into his brain stem, and although his hands sported four human fingers, instead of thumbs he had a pair of opposable piranhas. With his octo-brain he could think of eight different things at once, which made him a master strategist, and his piranha thumbs meant he was a formidable opponent in close-quarters combat. His one weakness was a reliance upon special breathing equipment. He needed to be connected to an air tank or he'd be as floppy as a stunned haddock. All we had to do was cut off his air supply. The next few minutes would witness an epic battle between the forces of good (me and Serge) and the evil commander.

The fate of the world was in my hands.

Commander Octolux looked up from the control panel, threw back his bulbous head, and opened his vicious beak to let out a great, gurgling laugh. Somehow he knew we were coming—we had walked into a trap. His watery gaze fell upon me, that horrifying beak opened once more, and he said, "Luke, I'm not telling you again—your dinner's on the table."

Commander Octolux sounded a lot like my mom.

I glanced over my shoulder. Mom stood in my bedroom doorway. Even without an octo-brain and piranha hands, she was a fearsome presence.

"Luke, Luke—he is launching *le* missile!" Serge yelled over the headset. "Ah, *mon brave*, we are too late."

I turned back to the TV screen just in time to witness an animation of Octolux's missile rising from its undersea silo and shooting out of the ocean depths to wreak jellyfish doom upon the world. I threw down my game controller and sighed.

There were no save points on the final level, which meant we'd have to start again from the beginning, and those platypus mines at the first air lock had been a total pain to get past. Especially since Serge found the word *platypus* so funny that he kept forgetting not to step on the mines.

"I think that's enough *Star Guy* for one day," said Mom, switching off the console.

My parents had been so amazed and stunned and happy about avoiding the recent asteroid apocalypse that when I asked them shortly afterward for a new video game console, they'd not only agreed but also let me keep it in my bedroom. I'm not proud of taking advantage of them in their moment of weakness. On the other hand— brand-new Xbox!

"It's not *Star Guy*," I said. "It's *Star Guy 2: Danger from the Deep.*" There were two video games featuring the world's first real superhero, Star Guy. The first one was rushed out after he'd stopped Earth from being flattened by Nemesis. It was OK, but the sequel was better. However, both suffered from the same problem: they didn't feel real. For a start, neither was set in our town. Even worse was how they portrayed Star Guy. For example, in *Danger from the Deep,* Star Guy's secret identity is millionaire schoolboy Lance Launceston, who is bestowed with superpowers after an accident with a plasma generator at his father's fusion laboratory. He has kinetic blast power, and a Star Jet that can do Mach 6.

All of which is complete nonsense.

And how do I know this? Because Star Guy is Zack

Parker, who was given his powers by an alien named Zorbon the Decider. He gets $6.50 a week for his allowance, and has just regular telekinesis and a Carrera Vengeance mountain bike. And he's my big brother.

I slipped off my chair and followed Mom downstairs. I had played a small but, I like to think, key role in Zack's epic world-saving triumph, but no one was making video games about me. Perhaps because, apart from my best friend, Serge, and my neighbor (but definitely *not* girlfriend) Lara Lee, no one knew how I'd helped rescue Star Guy from the clutches of wannabe superhero and comic book store owner Christopher Talbot. But even if they had known, who wants to play a video game from the point of view of an eleven-year old boy with flat feet and no superpowers? It wouldn't be very popular. In fact, I don't think *I'd* play a video game as me.

As I trudged downstairs for dinner I heard a *tuk-tuk* noise from the hallway, and a small shape slid from the shadows beneath the hall table. A red squirrel waited for me at the foot of the stairs. I knew it was for me, since this wasn't the first time. The squirrel sat up on its hind legs and held out a note. It hadn't written the note—that would be silly—but I knew who had. As soon as I took the folded paper, it scurried off, its bushy tail bobbing back into the shadows.

"Assemble tonight," read the message, which was

scrawled in the familiar purple ink of a uni-ball Gelstick Pen with a 0.4 mm tip.

Just two little words, but they signified something big. Finally! Things had been quiet since the whole Star-Guy-Christopher-Talbot-volcano-comic-store-giant-asteroid business in the summer, and my life had returned to its dull routine. I scrunched the paper in my fist. All that was about to change. Something was in the air. I sniffed. Some kind of fishy thing in a goopy sauce. But that didn't matter, because something else was out there waiting for me. Something thrilling. Something danger-ous. Adventure was in the air, and its name was . . .

S.C.A.R.F.

DON'T GO OUT WITHOUT YOUR S.C.A.R.F.

After dinner I snuck out to the tree house in our backyard. When Dad and Grandpa put it up, they had no idea that the exact spot they'd chosen was a doorway between our world and a parallel world, or that it was destined to become the international headquarters for a secret superhero crime fighting organization known as S.C.A.R.F., or possibly S.P.A.T.U.L.A.—we hadn't yet decided, which was partly why we were meeting up tonight. There was a lot to discuss.

As I huffed and puffed to the top of the rope ladder, I reflected on recent events. Thanks to a catastrophically timed pee break, I had missed out on being granted my greatest wish: to become a superhero. As if that wasn't bad enough, it had happened twice.

Twice.

The second time, the powers were given to my neighbor, school friend and cub reporter Lara Lee. Now, instead of splashing the story of Star Guy across the front of the school newspaper, she had become the story. Right away, she and Zack teamed up to fight crime and have thrilling adventures. Which was very nice for them, but left Serge and me twiddling our game controllers. That's what this evening was about.

For weeks I'd been trying to get both superheroes in a room with us to discuss forming a team. Serge and I hoped to convince them that dynamic duos were old-fashioned, and that modern superheroes have a whole bunch of people helping them out in the background. Of course, usually they're ex–Special Forces commandos or genius-level scientists, not eleven-year-old boys with no practical skills, whose only expertise lies in knowing that the Hulk comic book character was meant to be gray and that Superman was originally bald. But we weren't going to mention that part.

Serge was already in the tree house, the first to arrive. He looked up as I entered, and I saw that his cheeks were covered in a bright red rash. "I am allergic to squirrel fur," he explained miserably. "I wish she would stop sending messages by small woodland creature."

"She's just exploring her new power," I said, sitting down next to him to wait for the others.

"I should warn you that I have taken an antihistamine," he added, "but I am unsure if it was drowsy or nondrowsy."

Serge and I had been through a lot together, most of it accompanied by a chocolate bar and an asthma inhaler. We were alike in many ways, but most of all we shared a passion for superheroes. I was as close to Serge as I used to be to my brother—though it's not that I don't get along with Zack; we're just in different places in our lives. I'm saving for the new Batman video game, and he's saving the world.

"Did you bring the designs?" I asked.

Serge unzipped a black portfolio case. We'd spent ages coming up with the name of our crime-fighting team, and even longer creating designs for the logo. I held up the first one, all sleek silver and black lettering, with a drop shadow that made it pop off the page. "Nice," I cooed.

"Nice?" He seemed offended. "It is a highly effective design, at once simple and resonant with our target audience. Regard the swoosh, which adds dynamism, and the bold use of chiaroscuro—"

"The what?"

He sighed. "Light and shade, Luke. Light. And. Shade."

I held up the second design side by side with the first. "I'm still not sure about these. S.C.A.R.F. and S.P.A.T.U.L.A. aren't exactly fearsome, awe-inspiring acronyms."

When the title letters of a phrase spell out a word,

it's called an acronym. We'd tried to create one as cool as S.H.I.E.L.D. or T.H.U.N.D.E.R., but it's much harder than it looks.

There was a rustle of leaves from outside the tree house, and a moment later Star Guy blew through the doorway to land before us with a controlled thud. He struck a pose, head down, one knee on the floor, one arm trailing behind him, cape settling across his back. Slowly, he lifted his masked face. These days Zack rarely just arrived anywhere—he made an *entrance*.

I could tell without looking beside me that Serge was impressed. Even though he had played a vital role in the Nemesis adventure, Serge hadn't yet outgrown the fan-boy phase. On a daily basis, I was rather less in awe of Zack. It's hard to be impressed when you get the blame for a messy room and can't say it's because your brother threw a telekinetic fit looking for his spare cape.

Ah yes, the cape.

For ages Zack wouldn't wear a proper costume, saying that a mask and cape looked stupid, but in the end he came around. Zack is a bit skinny, and the billowing cape gives him more presence. The mask guards his identity, but it also protects the delicate skin around his eyes. He was getting some serious windburn from all that flying.

There was a flutter and a hoot from the doorway as Lara glided into the tree house. She didn't have the same flying superpower as Star Guy; instead, she relied on a unique propulsion system.

Birds.

They clung to her sleeves and pant legs: geese for altitude, pigeons for guidance, and frantically flapping sparrows for maneuvering. She touched down gently, extending one poised foot to the floor and then the other. Landing accomplished, she chirped at the birds. Releasing their grip on her, they streamed from the tree house back out into the night.

The superpower that Zorbon the Decider had given Lara was the ability to command animals. Not all animals: tigers, elephants, polar bears—basically anything big and fearsome—didn't respond to her. We'd been to the zoo and had checked. It was only creatures like squirrels and rabbits and small birds that she could control, which I couldn't help thinking was, well, kind of lame.

And then there was her costume. It was unlike any other, which is to say that it covered her body in a sensible fashion. Whenever I look at girl superheroes in comics, my first thought is that if they went out wearing so little clothing, they would catch a chill. And one day I'd like someone to explain to me the point of an armored bikini. Anyway, I'd helped Lara decide on her costume. So, in addition to a mask and cape, she wore a tough leather jacket, dark pants with useful zip pockets, gloves for protection from claws, and big black boots.

She'd also needed my help choosing her superhero name. Obviously it had to be animal-based, so she suggested names like Talon, Claw, and Birdgirl.

"All taken," I informed her.

"What about something with *wing?*"

"There's already a Nightwing," I said.

"Then I could be Daywing!" said Lara.

I frowned. "That sounds like part of a hospital."

In the end she decided to call herself Flutter, which, according to my comic collection, was still available. It was also terrible, but at first she wouldn't budge. After a great deal of persuasion, she finally agreed to *Dark* Flutter, which added a hint of fear to the featheriness. Although Serge thought it sounded like a chocolate spread. He'd had to go make himself a sandwich.

In the tree house, Lara and Zack began to catch up on the past week's heroics, talking about events Serge and I knew nothing about, or had only seen reported on the news. It was as if we weren't even in the room.

Lara snapped her fingers. "Oh, I forgot to mention the—"

"Genetically modified grocery clerk?" finished Zack. "Taken care of." He brushed off a piece of glowing broccoli that had stuck to his sleeve.

"Oh, good."

"And those trapped miners?" he asked in return.

"Yes, the moles were a great idea. Thanks," said Lara, making a feverish burrowing motion with her hands.

Zack lifted his mask. It settled on his forehead with a twang of elastic. "No problem."

"By the way," said Lara, "great job on that evil artificial intelligence in JCPenney."

Zack shrugged. "Couldn't have done it without you, *partner*."

She gave him a friendly punch on the arm. "Stop it. You're embarrassing me."

They grinned at each other, distinctly pleased with their week's work.

"So," I said, "evil artificial intelligence, eh? Sounds like the kind of mission, say, where you could have used some backup?"

"Nah, we had it covered. Isn't that right, Dark Flutter?" Zack held up a palm, and Lara smacked a high five. He turned to me. "So, why have you brought us here? I have math homework, and it's polynomials."

I got straight to the point. "We're here to discuss the formation of a super-secret organization dedicated to fighting crime." I held up the logo designs. "S.C.A.R.F. is the Superhero Covert Alliance Reaction Force, and S.P.A.T.U.L.A. stands for Superhero PATrol United—"

"Is this for one of your role-playing game thingies?" Zack interrupted with a frown.

"No, it's nothing like that. It's real." I could see from his expression that he wasn't getting it.

Lara studied Serge's expertly shaded logo. "Bold use of Enrico Caruso," she said with a pitying smile. She was always muddling her words. Muddled or not, unlike my annoying big brother, she could tell I was miffed.

"Wait," said Zack, realization dawning. "*You* want to help *us* fight crime?"

Now we were getting somewhere. "Exactly."

He folded his arms. "Not a chance."

"But you need us!"

"Do we?"

He was forgetting an important point. "Who rescued you when you were abducted by Christopher Talbot, aka the Quintessence?"

"You just won't let it go, will you?" The muscles in his jaw clenched. "I get nabbed by a supervillain *one time*. It won't happen again."

"It's not fair!" I burst out. "You get superpowers. She gets superpowers. And what do I get? A pair of slip-on loafers!" I was breathing heavily. "Just hear us out, Zack, please."

My brother relented. "OK, OK, if it means so much to you."

I turned to Serge. "Ready?"

He sat cross-legged on the floor, head slumped on his chest, snoring lightly.

I sighed. "He took the drowsy." No matter. I could do this without him. It'd be just like my presentation to the class on wasps. Except hopefully without the mass breakout and the screaming. I jumped to my feet, clasped my hands behind my back, and began to pace. "Superheroes are in constant danger of making easily avoidable mistakes. If only Superman had had someone to tell him, 'Kal-El, step away from the glowing green rock.' That's why you need someone like me." I glanced down at the snuffling Serge. "And him."

Zack and Lara stood in silence. I could tell they weren't buying it. But I wasn't finished yet. "While I admit that you have gained *some* experience of how to be superheroes, you're still new to the job. On the other hand, I have *years* of experience. I've been reading comics since I was knee-high to Ant-Man."

Zack tutted. "Comics are useless. They don't tell you how to be a superhero."

Was he nuts? That's precisely what comics do. But just as I was about to say so, he cut me off. "Oh, sure, they're full of fantastic adventures, but they don't tell you about the *reality*. They don't tell you that you need to wear a vest to keep warm when flying at altitude. Or that under certain atmospheric conditions your telepathic power picks up NPR. Or that it's all very well to stop criminals, but you have to be very careful not to breach their civil rights or you open yourself up to accusations of unlawful restraint and wrongful arrest."

He was right—none of that stuff was in any comic I'd read. Probably because it sounded really boring. I turned to Dark Flutter. "Lara, come on. Who stopped you from choosing a dry-clean-only costume?"

"That's true." She nodded. "But there's quite a difference between reading washing instructions and fighting crime."

This was too much. "Well, you're a terrible superhero," I fumed. "Your power is *lame*."

"Lame?!" Lara placed her hands on her hips, raised her chin, and declared, "I have dominion over the animal kingdom."

"You have dominion over a petting zoo! In fact, you're not a superhero at all; you're a *Disney princess*."

She bristled with indignation, and I was glad she didn't have a spare hedgehog on hand.

"Maybe if you were ex–Special Forces or genius-level scientists we could team up," mused Zack.

"But, Zack—"

"Forget it. It's too dangerous. We've got superpowers; all you've got is a swooshy logo." I was about to protest when he clutched a hand to his forehead. "I'm picking up a disturbance on my Star Screen."

"I came up with that name," I muttered, but he ignored me.

"Someone's in trouble," he said. "Dark Flutter?"

"Right behind you, Star Guy." She cupped a hand to her mouth and squawked. In seconds the tree house filled with birds. "See you at school," she said to me as the birds picked her up.

I could only stand by and watch as she and Zack flew off on their next adventure.

There was a snort as Serge stirred and sat up. He looked around the tree house through bleary eyes. "Ah, zut, I missed them. So," he asked, turning to me, "Is it S.P.A.T.U.L.A.? Oh, I hope it is S.P.A.T.U.L.A."

MY GYM TEACHER IS A SUPERVILLAIN

"I'm not picking Luke Parker, miss. He's terrible."

There was a chortle from the rest of Miss Dunham's seventh-grade gym class. I sat unhappily on the bench beside Serge as our amused classmates formed two neat lines along one edge of the field. Forget joining an ultra-secret superhero team; we couldn't even get picked for soccer.

The October sun beat down on the Astroturf as the class divided into opposing sides. We were the last two to be chosen, as always. I found it maddening, but Serge didn't care. He said soccer was a trawler and they were all seagulls following the trawler, or we were the trawler and they were waiting for us to throw them sardines. Or something. I think it must have made more sense in French.

A screeching whistle pierced the air. It belonged to Miss Dunham, a terrifying woman with a voice like her whistle and bulgy eyes that reminded me of a praying mantis. She swiveled her insect gaze to the boy who had called me terrible. "Joshpal Khan," she began. "Yes, Luke and Serge might not be the most naturally gifted athletes the world has ever seen, and it's certainly true that Luke couldn't find the back of the goal with a GPS and a bloodhound, but that's no reason to be rude. Now choose."

Josh Khan thought for a moment. "Can I pick the bench?"

The rest of the class dissolved into whooping laughter. I noticed the corner of Miss Dunham's mouth curling into a small smile. I didn't take it personally, because I knew what this was really about.

My gym teacher was a supervillain.

"Ah, *mon ami*, as much as I am eager to believe, I do not think that is likely," said Serge. It was ten minutes later, and we were huddled together on the touchline. Occasionally a pack of our classmates would rush past, loudly chasing a ball.

"But her first name is *Susan*," I said.

"Uh, and how exactly does that make her the supervillain?"

"You're not getting it. Susan Dunham. Sue Dunham. *Pseudonym!*"

Serge gazed at me blankly. "I do not know this word."

For a comic book mega-fan, Serge could be surprisingly ignorant. "A pseudonym is when you give yourself a false name to protect your true identity. Y'know, like the Riddler is Edward Nygma. E. Nygma. *Enigma*. Or Walter E. Go, which was the *alter ego* of Christopher Talbot." Figuring that out had put us on the track of the villainous comic store owner.

Mulling this fresh insight, Serge studied Miss Dunham across the field. She scuttled on spindly legs after the high-pitched pack of players, who were now streaming in the opposite direction. "Have you considered that per'aps she is a super*hero*, not a villain? Heroes also use sue-dunhams."

"No chance." I shook my head. "Let's examine the evidence," I said. "Number one: last week, when she was demonstrating her basketball speed dribble, she knocked Oliver Johnson to the ground." Serge gave me a puzzled look. "To accomplish her objectives she is willing to harm innocent bystanders," I explained. "That's classic supervillain behavior. Number two: she appeared *mysteriously* on the first day of the semester—"

"I believe she appeared in a Volkswagen Bug."

"And she promptly *stole* Miss McCann's parking spot. See—she will stop at nothing!" I could tell that Serge wasn't entirely swayed, but I had yet to hit him with the big one. "And number three, the most conclusive proof of all: you, Serge. *You*."

"*Moi?*"

"You have a note from your *maman*, correct?"

"Yes, I am not supposed to exert myself," he said.

"And what did Miss Dunham do when you presented it to her?"

"Miss Dunham ripped it up."

"She doesn't care. She doesn't care about your note." Serge paused. "She is evil."

"That's what I'm saying."

He shielded his eyes from the low sun. "So, what then is Miss Dunham's fiendish master plan?"

"I'm glad you asked me that." We watched her use a supervillain's lightning reflexes to duck Ed Stansfield's pinpoint free kick. "Well, at first I thought she might be attempting to unleash some ancient brooding evil buried for millennia beneath the school. That would explain the dark, horrible atmosphere I feel when I walk down the corridors and sit in the classrooms. But then I realized . . . that might just be me."

Serge laid a consoling hand on my shoulder. The first semester of junior high had been harder than I'd expected. I may have helped save the planet from certain destruction during summer vacation, but no one knew. And even when I'd dropped a few hints about my involvement with Star Guy, instead of being impressed, the other kids gave me odd looks and whispered things like "pathetic" and "weirdo" behind my back in the lunch line. It felt as if everyone else at school knew exactly what they were doing, had somewhere to go, and had someone to go there with. Of course, I had Serge, but apart from PE we didn't share any classes, so I only saw him at recess. And even if I hadn't annoyed Lara, she was too busy being Dark Flutter to hang out.

I'd been hoping for a break, and it looked like I was about to get one. The school's janitor had found some weird mold infesting the gym. Even though it was unlikely to be anything interesting, like an invading alien spore, the principal was taking no chances. School would be closed all through next week while the fumigators nuked it. For me that meant one blissful week without Josh Khan and the hooting laughter of my classmates.

Miss Dunham furiously waved a yellow card in Parminder Chaudry's face.

"Per'aps she is one of those villains who seek to create the perfect world," suggested Serge. "She has looked around her at the chaos and misunderstanding, and it displeases her. So she plans to bring about order and discipline by making everyone do laps around the playing field and climb the rope." He shook his head slowly at this terrible vision of the future. "I do not want to live in a world like that."

But Serge was wrong. I knew her plan, and it was even worse than his grim prediction. "She's targeting Star Guy."

"*Non*. But how do you know?" said Serge.

"There is a list on the wall in her office. It is headed 'Most Wanted.' Can you guess the name at the very top of that list? Zack Parker. Somehow she's discovered his secret identity."

Serge flinched. "Ah no, she has spotted us."

From the right back position deep in the other side of the field, Miss Dunham's insect vision latched on to us like a frog's sticky tongue on a fly. "Quick," I muttered, "pretend you're offside."

"Too late," cried Serge.

Miss Dunham's whistle shrilled across the field. She raised one tracksuited arm and yelled, "Hey, you two, get in the game. What are you afraid of?" A cruel smile flashed on her lips. "If you mess up your hair, it won't be the end of the world."

Serge and I exchanged looks. *The end of the world?* Could this be even worse than I'd feared? Perhaps we weren't dealing with just any low-level supervillain. Perhaps the greatest threat to our existence since the Nemesis asteroid was wearing a light-blue tracksuit and wielding an Acme Thunderer silver-plated whistle.

"Well, what do you say now?" I asked, walking onto the field to the jeers and slow clapping of our classmates.

At my side, Serge stared straight ahead, stone-faced. "She must be stopped."

"Well, the good news is that Miss Dunham's ankle is *not* broken," said the principal. It was later that same afternoon, and Serge and I sat opposite him in his office. He had a head like a tomato, and his name was Hines—an unfortunate combination. He loomed behind a desk the size of an Imperial Star Destroyer, his gaze like a tractor beam. "However, you two boys are in a great deal of trouble."

"But she has a 'Most Wanted' list," I blurted. "It's on her wall, with my brother's name circled in blood."

Mr. Hines frowned. "I would hazard a guess it's ballpoint, Luke, and I believe Miss Dunham wants your brother for the track team. He's her number one target."

"Oh, come on, sir." I scoffed. "Are we really supposed to believe *that?*"

He leaned in, his big ripe head filling my vision. "What *do* you believe, Luke?"

That our gym teacher has been hiding her true, hideous form behind the human mask of Sue Dunham and is actu-

ally an insectoid supervillain with plans for global domination. I shrugged. "Don't know, sir."

Mr. Hines sighed. "You don't know. Of course not."

It began to appear that my suspicions about Miss Dunham had been misplaced. Unfortunately, I was only coming to this realization *after* catching her in the swiftly devised and brilliantly executed Operation Venus Flytrap. Over lunch Serge and I had set a cunning trap in her natural habitat: the school gym. The trap involved a pair of portable basketball hoops, a large net, a ball cage, a scoreboard, and a lot of mini-trampolines. It had worked beautifully. Miss Dunham had ended up wrapped in the net, squished into the ball cage. She made a lot of fuss in a high-pitched squeal that sounded to me like just the sort of thing you'd hear from an insect-based supervillain. Phase two of our plan was simple. We waited for her to shed her human skin and reveal her true pincer-snapping, hairy-legged form.

We were still waiting when her next class arrived for volleyball.

Now, Mr. Hines sat back. His leather chair creaked like my grandpa's knees.

"You'd do well to take a page from your big brother's book. Zack Parker is a shining example of responsibility, diligence, and academic excellence."

I wanted to scream. Instead I wriggled in my chair

and seethed like a bubbling volcano.

"Now, I don't believe that either of you boys *meant* to hurt Miss Dunham. However, that doesn't excuse your behavior. Miss Dunham herself has suggested your punishment."

Banished to the Phantom Zone? Locked up in Arkham Asylum?

"When school resumes, in addition to your regular PE schedule, you will both be required to run twenty laps around the playing field and climb the rope, twice a week."

Serge went pale, mumbled something in French, and took a quick suck from his asthma inhaler. Mr. Hines said some more stuff about responsibility and conduct and top buttons on shirts, then sent us back to class.

"Sue Dunham." Out in the corridor I shook my head, mystified at my error of judgment. "But I was so sure. . . ."

"Face it, Luke—she is not the supervillain. Not even a regular villain." Serge sighed. "I bet her name is not even Susan."

"But all the evidence . . ."

He pursed his lips and blew out. "It was wishful thinking. We have been so desperate to experience a new adventure that we see evil everywhere." He looked at me. "Per'aps it is time for us to put those wishes behind us. My *maman* says now that I have commenced junior high,

I am poised on the edge of a bigger world."

I frowned. "Middle-earth?"

"Yes, I asked that too. But it is not what she meant," said Serge. "She explained that the world she refers to is strange and yet familiar, full of opportunity and disappointment, love and heartache. And now that it is before us, there is no turning back." He stopped at a classroom door. "I have drama." Without saying another word, he went inside for an hour of mime and improv. I shrugged off a creeping sense of unease. I was confident he'd get over his *maman*'s frankly bonkers statement and we'd be back to rooting out supervillains in no time.

As I went off to math class, I turned the corner and collided with Lara. We hadn't spoken since my outburst in the tree house, when I'd accused her of being a souped-up Snow White, so I was relieved when she saw me and smiled.

"Hi, Luke," she said. "You wouldn't believe the morning I've had! *Three* airplanes suffered catastrophic electrical faults, all at the same time." She put out a hand and glided it downward, making a jet sound. "But you should've seen Zack. Whoosh, bosh, zap! I barely needed to use my pigeons at all. I'll tell you all about it later. Don't want to be late for class."

"Sure," I said dismally.

"What's wrong?" She paused, lifting a hand to search

her hair. "I don't have a hedgehog in there *again*, do I?"

"No. No hedgehog."

"Luke, are you OK?"

"I'm fine. Firing on all thrusters," I said, forcing a smile. "I'm sorry for calling you a lame superhero."

"That's OK," she said. "I know you didn't mean it."

The truth was, I kind of did. A part of me was relieved that I had missed Zorbon's latest visit, when he had given her such a silly superpower.

Lara shuffled her feet and smiled at me shyly. "Luke, I want to tell you something. It's kind of . . . awkward. It's not something I expected to say to you, but—"

Just then, two kids from her English class swung past, and Lara looked alarmed. Her tone changed. "Oh, I'm going to be late. Gotta shoot," she said, hurrying off. "We should do lunch," she called over her shoulder. "It's veggie lasagna in the cafeteria tomorrow." And with that she turned the corner and was gone.

I stood in the empty corridor, thinking over what she'd just said. Apart from her acting all weird, two things bothered me. One, I hated veggie lasagna. Two, airplanes didn't fall out of the sky for no reason.

THE SALMON FILLET OF DOOM

"No more *Star Guy* for you, Luke Alfred Parker."

When Mom discovered what had happened at school, she hit the roof. She marched into my bedroom and removed the Xbox, informing me that I could have it back at the end of the break, *if* I managed to stay out of trouble until then. Brilliant. First no S.C.A.R.F., and now no video games. I considered getting down on my knees and pleading, but I knew it would do no good. Mom was as likely to change her mind as the Joker was to start performing at children's parties.

She wouldn't let me near the computer in the living room either, which made it impossible to probe the mystery of the plummeting airplanes. I was reduced to watching the news on TV like someone from the olden days.

Annoyingly, the midair rescue was even more amazing than Lara had made it sound. As usual these days, every moment had been caught on multiple camera phones. First, you see the landing lights of the three planes as they line up for the runway. Then there's a flash and the planes suddenly drop.

The TV newspeople had overlaid the pictures with the conversation between the pilots and air traffic control. So as the first plane nosedives, you hear, "Control Tower, this is Delta Two Four. Experiencing catastrophic power loss to both engines. Attempting restart. Mayday. Mayday." Before the control tower can respond, you hear the other two pilots call in the exact same Mayday from their cockpits.

There was even video from inside the planes. The passengers are screaming and crying. The man holding the camera phone is desperately recording a message for his children. Saying good-bye. It's awful.

And then . . .

"Look!" shouts the woman in the seat beside him, pointing a shaking finger at the window. The man turns his phone. At first you can't see anything, but suddenly there, dropping through the clouds at three hundred miles per hour, streaking to the rescue, it's . . .

"Star Guy!" cries the woman.

"And . . . the other one!" shouts the man.

The coverage switches back to the outside of the planes. You see Star Guy approaching, cape fluttering in the wind, sun glinting off his sigil. He loops around the wings, containing the failing engines with his force field; then he uses his telekinetic power to stop the planes' rapid descent. Dark Flutter dispatches pigeons to the wingtips, steadying the aircraft. Then Star Guy flies alongside the cockpit of the first aircraft and throws the pilots a salute, before leading them in for a perfect landing.

Inside, the passengers' screams turn to whoops of excitement. The man with the camera is crying, telling his kids that he'll see them soon.

Even I had to admit that my brother was getting the hang of this superhero business. The salute was a particularly nice touch.

"Those passengers were very lucky," said Mom, wiping away a tear as we watched them slide down the emergency chutes onto the runway in front of a line of waiting ambulances and fire engines.

Statistically, she couldn't have been more wrong. The chances of three modern airplanes going down like that at precisely the same moment in the same airspace were infinitesimally low. That's what made it so suspicious. "What do you mean?" I asked.

"If that had happened anywhere else in the world, Star Guy wouldn't have been around to save them."

I hadn't thought of that. Mom was right. Could it be a coincidence, or did it point to something more significant? If I was going to investigate, I needed the Internet.

"Mom, I really need the computer to do my homework."

"Really? Can't you use a wax tablet and a stylus like your dad and I had to?"

I think Mom was trying to be funny, since they only used wax tablets and styluses in ancient Greece. And they didn't have girls in school back then. And my mom wasn't 2,500 years old.

"Fine. You can use the computer," she relented. "But I'm installing a new security feature to make sure it's only for homework."

I sat down confidently in front of the screen. There wasn't any security software on the planet that I couldn't outwit.

Mom drew up a chair and planted herself down beside me.

OK. There was one.

There was the snick of a key turning in the front door. Zack tended to use his bedroom window these days, which meant it had to be Dad. He was home late from the office again. Mom and Dad both worked at a big insurance company in town. The company had had to pay out a lot of money following all the damage caused by the Nemesis asteroid. Even though Star Guy had stopped the main asteroid, he couldn't prevent hundreds of small chunks of rock getting through. They broke windows, cars—and even sank a ship. All of them were insurance claims. My parents had been working like crazy for weeks to clear the backlog.

Dad appeared in the living room doorway. He looked even more tired than usual. With his sunken eyes and pale, drawn complexion, he hovered on the threshold like a vampire unable to enter without an invitation. "Hey, Luke, good day at school?"

"Don't ask," said Mom, before I could reply.

He caught her eye and in one of those this-is-not-for-children's-ears voices said, "Can we have a chat?"

She turned to me and raised a warning finger. "When I come back I'm checking your history."

They disappeared into the kitchen, and I got to work. I wasn't worried about Mom checking my Internet history, since she'd find nothing. I was a ninja piloting a stealth fighter dipped in invisible ink.

As I started my search I couldn't help thinking about Lara. She was great at this kind of thing. I missed her. Back before she got her superpowers we could talk for ages, but now there was an invisible barrier between us. And not one of the cool ones. The kind that made it difficult to know what to say around her.

The results of my search were displayed before me. I found the news report I'd watched with Mom, and fast-forwarded to the moment just before the planes fell. I played through the section one frame at a time until I found what I was looking for. In the top left corner, half hidden by a cloud, was a flash of light.

"What are you up to?"

It was Zack. I'd been so focused that I hadn't heard him come in. He had shed his superhero costume and now wore regular clothes, although they were noticeably clean and pressed, and his hair was spiked with gel.

"I think you should see this," I said.

He yawned. "Can it wait? I'm completely zonked. After I stopped those planes from crashing, I had English with Mr. Bonnick. If you think catching three airplanes is hard . . ." He shook his head. "And then I was hanging out with Cara." He tugged at his collar and preened in the mirror.

Cara was Lara's older sister, and my brother had a crush on her that was stronger than the Hulk's grip. But he wasn't *hanging out* with her. At least, not the way he made it sound. Zack was tutoring her in physics, though he liked to pretend otherwise. Sadly for him, his crush only went one way. I may have been powerless, but I knew my brother's weak spots. *How's her boyfriend?* I thought. One of Zack's superpowers was telepathy—and being brothers, we had a special telepathic bond. So I knew my question would boom inside his head in surround sound, which would make it even more irritating.

"That's it!" he yelled, turning the same color as an enraged Commander Octolux. "One more inappropriate use of my telepathic power and I'm blocking you. Got it?"

He was overreacting. It wasn't as if I used our telepathic link for trivial reasons.

"Yes, you do," said Zack, reading my mind. "All the time! Last week you used it to ask me to pick up a bag of sour-cream-and-onion chips from the corner store."

"Well, we'd run out."

Zack threw up his hands in exasperation. "I wasn't even in the corner store! I was locked in fierce hand-to-hand combat with a man in a lion costume. Don't ask. But that wasn't your worst telepathic abuse, oh no. That would be when you used it to ask for answers during a math test."

Typical that my goody-goody brother would be wound up most by that.

He stomped to the door, muttering, "I'm the world's greatest superhero, and he uses me like a takeout menu and a *calculator.*"

"Zack, I'm sorry. Don't go. I think some sort of electromagnetic pulse weapon brought down those airplanes."

He raised one dubious eyebrow. "So tell me, this electro-magenta laser gun thingy—does it by any chance belong to your gym teacher?"

Ah. "You heard about that then."

"Um, yeah. The whole school heard. You're a laughingstock, Luke."

"But I was so sure Miss Dunham was evil," I complained. "All the evidence said so."

He thumbed at the photo on my screen. "And don't tell me—all the evidence here screams big bad supervillain."

It did. "No army, navy, or air force in the world has an electromagnetic pulse weapon capable of bringing down airplanes," I explained. "What's more, this one is airborne and, if the lack of reports is anything to go by, invisible to radar. It *has* to come from a technologically superior mind. If there isn't a supervillain behind this, I'll eat my limited-edition Crimson Avenger fedora."

Zack relented with a sigh. "OK, so show me this mysterious, flying, invisible gun then."

"There. That flash of light."

He leaned in, squinting at the screen. "You're kidding me, right? That's nothing. It's a light from another plane or a smudge on the camera lens, that's all."

"So why did those planes fall out of the sky?"

"How should I know? I can fly, but that doesn't make me an expert on airplane engineering. And you aren't one either. Just because you don't understand what happened doesn't mean you can jump to ridiculous conclusions." He shook his head sadly. "You can't go through life seeing supervillains everywhere."

There was no point trying to persuade him. After all, he wasn't the only superhero in the world anymore. Tomorrow I'd fill Lara in on my suspicions—even if I had to do it over veggie lasagna.

Mom called us in for dinner. The four of us ate in the kitchen together as usual. Zack might have been the one with superpowered senses, but as soon as I took my seat, I could tell that something was wrong. A cloud hung over the table, and it wasn't coming from the steamed rice. I didn't have to wait long to learn the bad news.

Dad had lost his job with the insurance company.

"Did they fire you because you disobeyed orders and went rogue?" I asked.

"Unfortunately not, Luke," he said, picking at his food with a fork. "Nothing as exciting as that. With all the money the company has had to pay out because of Nemesis, they're having to cut back."

Zack sat up. "But that's not fair," he said. "Nemesis was, what do you call it, an 'act of god'?"

"You're right," said Dad. "But all those chunks of asteroid that broke off when Star Guy stopped Nemesis— well, they were an act of man, albeit a superhuman one, and they smashed houses and cars. Those were claims."

I looked over at my brother. He was clenching his fists so tightly they'd turned white.

"I'm just a victim of downsizing," said Dad. He lifted his fork. "Which, before you ask, yes, is *exactly* like a shrink ray." He gave a short laugh. Mom laid her hand on his.

I knew that downsizing was nothing like a shrink ray. Shrink rays were expensive and complicated, and the idea that an insurance company would use one to fire people was ridiculous. The electricity bill alone would make it uneconomic. I looked around at the concerned faces at the table. Everyone was thinking the same thing, but no one wanted to ask. It was up to me. "So," I began, choosing my words with care, "will you get another job, or are you going to be hanging around the house from now on?"

"Luke!" Mom snapped.

"You idiot!" Zack punched me in the arm.

Dad just laughed. "Don't you worry about me, Luke. That job was like the Hobbit movies: it went on *way* too long. A fresh start will be good for me. I can't wait to see what the future has in store. Bring it on!"

And then he sighed and looked down at his salmon fillet.

THE BREAKING OF THE FELLOWSHIP

It was the last hour of the last day before the fumigation break. The corridors swarmed with students heading to their final classes before one precious and unexpected week off. I hadn't seen Serge all day. I finally caught up with him and we were carried along in the noisy surge. Serge had geography and I had art, so we were going our separate ways. I was about to learn that that was true in more ways than one.

"What do you mean, you can't come over?" I said. "We have important S.C.A.R.F. business to discuss."

Serge gave me an awkward look. "It is my *maman*. After the business with Miss Dunham, she says that you are a bad influence and I must avoid you."

"Avoid *me*?" I was outraged.

"*Oui.* I have been wanting to tell you all day, but it is difficult for me. You are my best friend, and you are a sensitive soul."

"I'm not sensitive," I snapped. "Or a bad influence. I'm harmless. Well, *mostly* harmless."

"I know. That is what *I* said. Luke Parker may appear to be full of confidence and *le* smart aleck, but scratch the surface and beneath you will encounter an anxious boy who simply wants to be accepted."

"I wouldn't have put it quite like that," I mumbled.

We were approaching the geography classroom. "There was talk at the dinner table that I should move to another school," said Serge quietly. "I would not even mention it, but it was over the cheese course."

This was awful. Serge was not only my best friend; he was currently my only friend. I'd gone to meet Lara at lunchtime in order to tell her my theory about what had brought down the airplanes, but she hadn't showed, no doubt off saving some old people from a burning retirement home. What with her bailing on me to go and be Dark Flutter, if Serge left, then I'd be that kid at the back of the school cafeteria eating his sandwiches alone.

Serge couldn't look me in the eye. "I am sorry," he said. "Truly."

I could still rescue the situation. After all, he and I had faced the end of the world together and come out the other side. Nothing could separate us, not even his *maman*. All I had to do was find the right words.

"Fine," I said sharply. "I don't need you either." With

that I marched off along the corridor and didn't look back.

Lara sent a vole with an apology. I opened the note in the tree house, where I had retreated as soon as I got home from my bruising day at school. I was alone, apart from a heaped plate of crustless peanut butter sandwiches and a double-chocolate milkshake. And the vole.

The note confirmed my earlier suspicions. Lara had missed our lunch meeting because of superhero commitments. She'd written that she would try to pop by later, but her mom was taking her to buy new shoes. That said it all. I came a distant second to a pair of ballet flats. First Serge, now Lara. And forget about Zack; he'd been far too important to pay me any attention for ages.

The vole sat on the floor, gazing up. I could swear it looked sorry for me.

"What are you waiting for?" I asked. "A tip?"

The vole said nothing.

"Well, I'll give you a tip," I said, taking a bite of sandwich. "Stay away from owls. Got it?"

The vole looked at me blankly.

"Because they're your natural predators," I explained as I chewed.

I sighed. Not even voles were interested in what I had to say. I waved my half-eaten sandwich. "Know what I don't get?"

The vole did not.

"Zorbon the Decider, that's what. First time he rolls up, he hands out superpowers and a warning. *Nemesis is coming.* Oooh. Big scary end-of-the-world riddle. But the next time he shows his shiny, interdimensional head in here, what does he do? Turns Lara into a superpowered rodent-whisperer—no offense—and that's it. No warning. No strange prediction. Nothing." I paused to suck a mouthful of milkshake through twin straws. When I lowered the drink, the vole had gone. I poked my head out of the tree house to see it scurrying off into the garden.

"Zorbon doesn't hand out powers for nothing," I called after it. "So the question is, what kind of threat is so terrible it's going to take not one but *two* superheroes to deal with it? I'm telling you, something wicked is heading into town. Mark my words."

But no one did. Only the wind answered. Swirling in the oak tree, it shook the turning leaves, making them rattle like bones.

PUNY EARTHLINGS!

The break began with a bang—and a zap and an atomic *whump*. I threw off my comforter and went downstairs to investigate the pounding that was coming from the living room, to find Dad slumped on the sofa in front of the TV, playing on my video game console. Mom had already left for work, and Zack was at the library studying for exams he didn't have to take for another two years. I assumed that "going to the library" was code for "foiling a bank robbery" or "freeing the hostages," but with my super-nerd of a brother, you could never be sure.

Dad was wearing his bathrobe and the Hulk slippers I'd bought him for his last birthday (he looked less "Hulk smash" and more "Hulk shuffle with a cup of cocoa").

"Morning, son. And how are you this fine—oh, hang on." He broke off to repeatedly stab the FIRE button on the game controller. On-screen, a familiar building exploded in a cloud of radioactive dust.

"Isn't that the Walgreens on Main Street?" I asked.

"Uh-huh." Dad nodded, concentrating furiously on the game.

A video game set in our town? *Strange,* I thought. Then again, no stranger than a superhero living here. The empty box lay discarded on the floor. LAB RAT GAMES, read the logo on the side. I'd never heard of them. Rising out of the cover art—a colorful illustration of the suburbs in flames—was the title in big letters: *Puny Earthlings!* Dad must have bought it in town—the same town he was now gleefully turning to rubble. This was great. But then I remembered that Mom had imposed a thirty-foot exclusion zone around my Xbox. I took a step back.

"Where're you going?" asked Dad. "We can play together." He tossed me the second controller.

Well, OK then. If it was fine with Dad, then it was fine with me too. I slid onto the sofa beside him and jumped right into the game.

From what I could pick up playing through the Main Street level, it was a twist on the alien invasion story. Instead of fighting off hordes of attackers from outer space, *you* were the aliens. You could jump from the cockpit of a fighter-bomber to the bridge of the mile-long mother ship to the strategic brain of the Alien Overlord itself. Lab Rat Games had gone to town on the design. The graphics gleamed. Our town had never looked better—

apart from the craters and mass devastation, obviously.

The designers had not only lovingly re-created the town; they'd also reproduced its inhabitants. Individual faces were recognizable. There was the mayor, there the lady from the post office, over there the man who drove the ice-cream truck that was always parked outside our school in the afternoon.

"Don't you think this is all a bit . . . odd?" I said.

Dad didn't look up from the screen. "Attention to detail, son—that's what it is. Y'know, the thing almost entirely absent from your homework."

I ignored the insult. "Is that Mitali from down the block?" I leaned in. A small human figure zigzagged her way through the park, trying to shake off a squad of alien shock troops. "They've even got her Avengers backpack." *If Mitali is in this game,* I wondered, *could I be in it too?* Immediately I flew my assault craft down Moore Street and parked outside our house. I guided my alien warrior from the cockpit and lumbered up our driveway, disintegrated the front door, and barged inside.

My mom and dad stood in the hallway.

I burst out laughing. They looked just like the real thing, right down to the frowny expression Dad gets when he's reading an instruction manual.

"I don't remember giving permission for this," said Dad, on seeing his virtual self.

"No," I said, "but you have to admire the attention to detail."

He shot me a sideways look, and then his expression returned to one of puzzlement. "How did they get our images?"

I shrugged. "Maybe they took it from your library card?" I didn't care. It was so cool. I searched the house, but there was no sign of a virtual me. Zack, however, was in his bedroom reading a book. Typical. Dad stopped me from blasting him to ashes.

I brought up an on-screen menu and, with a couple of button pushes, jumped out of the soldier and into the Alien Overlord's character in the command ship. I returned to the important business of invading the planet.

The earthlings sent in their military. Battle tanks, attack helicopters, and strike fighters all fell before our superior alien weaponry. But just when I thought we couldn't lose came the next twist in the game.

Earth's greatest defenders showed up.

Star Guy and Dark Flutter swooped in, and before I knew it, they had kicked our alien bottoms back to Centaurus A.

The defeat triggered the final cut-scene animation showing what was left of the invasion fleet turning their green tails and fleeing the earth.

Dad turned to me, arched one eyebrow, and gurgled, "So, Admiral Flibol, Terror of the Ninth Quadrant, Vanquisher of the Lorbofloz Horde, Holder of the Order of the Shining Custard for Valor, shall we play again?"

We did. We played through the morning, four bowls of Cocoa Puffs, most of two large pizzas, a liter of Coke, a carton of Extremely Chocolaty Temptation ice cream, the entire box of Girl Scout cookies at the back of the cupboard that Mom thought we didn't know about (they were Tagalongs), a box of after-dinner mints individually wrapped in green foil that were a present, a can and a half of Pringles, and an apple (for nutritional balance).

As I launched yet another fiery invasion upon the panicking humans, I took a moment to admire another aspect of the game: the R & D laboratory (which Dad explained stood for "research and development" and not "railguns and Death Stars," though he did agree that in this case it could just as easily mean that). Here, deep in the heart of the Alien Overlord's mother ship, you used nanomachine replicators to design and build all kinds of weapons—from the obvious, like sonic blasters and thermal detonators, to the unusual, like a tank that you grew in a tank, and genetically mutated attack penguins. You could create almost anything you could imagine. It was like evil Minecraft.

Remembering how Zack had been weakened when he

was cut off from starlight, I cobbled together a weather weapon with the capability to turn the skies cloudy. But the game versions of Star Guy and Dark Flutter simply flew up through the clouds to recharge. (In real life, after what had happened with Christopher Talbot, Zack never went out unless he was at least half-charged, and always filled up at the end of each day. He was as careful about recharging as he was about handing in his homework on time.)

When Dad and I finally lowered our game controllers and lifted our bloodshot eyes from the screen, we saw that the devastation we'd brought to our virtual town was mirrored in our living room. A landfill's worth of cardboard packaging and scraps of food littered the carpet. On the wall, where the painting that Mom did at art school had hung, was a dusty outline and a nail. I vaguely remembered a crash behind me during the final ground assault on the mall, but had assumed it was due to the excellent surround sound.

Dad retrieved the painting from behind the sofa.

"Why didn't Mom do art instead of getting a job in insurance?"

Dad thought for a moment. "It's good to follow your dreams, but it doesn't always work out, and then you have to know when to stop. And that's tough." He traced a finger lightly over the painting before hanging it once again in its place on the wall.

"Dad, did you stop dreaming?"

He nodded slowly. "But it was much easier for me."

"Why? What did you want to be?"

He straightened the painting. "A Jedi knight."

That figured. Dad surveyed the wreckage of the living room. "We should probably get out the vacuum cleaner."

"Yeah, we probably should," I said.

"Or . . ." Dad's eyes swiveled to the TV. The game menu filled the screen, the START button pulsing like a neutron star. *"Puny earthlings!"* boomed a synthesized alien voice through the speakers.

"No. We can't," he said.

"No," I agreed.

"Ready, player one?" said Dad.

Amazingly, by the time Mom came home from work, there was no sign of our marathon gaming session. The carpet, which at one point had disappeared beneath a mountain of debris, was now entirely visible, and the bottle of I Can't Believe It Was Butter stain remover had proved remarkably effective with the Extremely Chocolaty Temptation spills. I caught her briefly inspecting her painting on the wall, but if she had any suspicions, they didn't last long. Dad had prepared dinner as a distraction. When I'd asked him earlier what he was making, he replied, "Tactical shepherd's pie."

Zack called to say we shouldn't wait for him, because he was—and I quote—"staying late at the library." Your guess is as good as mine.

I'd enjoyed playing *Puny Earthlings!* with Dad. There was just one problem. Despite spending the whole day devising more and more outrageous strategies, we had failed to overcome the combined forces of Star Guy and Dark Flutter. The game was simple. You couldn't win until you'd neutralized Earth's superheroes.

All through dinner I could think of nothing else. I knew it wasn't merely the challenge of the game that made me burn to brush Star Guy and Dark Flutter aside. Defeated by them in the virtual world, I had also been rejected by them in the real world. And it stung worse than my unfortunate wasp presentation. As I brushed my teeth, I made a decision. While I couldn't get one over on them in real life, I resolved to crush them in the game.

As I slipped into bed, I suddenly remembered the airplanes and my suspicions about an electromagnetic super-weapon. I turned off the light and watched the tree shadows moving on my ceiling. Maybe Zack was right and there was no weapon. And even if some super-villain *was* lurking behind the incident, what could I do?

Zack and Lara weren't interested, S.C.A.R.F. hadn't made it past the logo stage, and even Serge wasn't talking to me. I was on my own.

No one else cared, so why should I? I decided to forget all about it. Instead, I planned to enjoy my week off school by taking over the world.

THE DEATH OF SUPERMAN

How do you defeat a superhero?

I pondered the question as I rode the bus to Main Street. I needed inspiration and decided to look for it in Crystal Comics. I hadn't been back since the whole Nemesis business during the summer. As I stepped off the 55 and looked over the familiar storefront, I felt a pang of regret. The last time I'd been here was with Serge and Lara. That wasn't the only difference.

Christopher Talbot, the owner (and supervillain), hadn't been seen since he was swatted out of the sky by a giant asteroid going 27,000 miles per hour. Since his disappearance, his business empire had rapidly dwindled. His former villain's lair and flagship volcano store had lain empty for little more than a month before signs went up announcing it as the future location of a new Macy's. In the absence of their charismatic owner, the dozen or so stores that made up the Crystal Comics empire were snapped up by a competitor. The original store on Main Street limped on, the last creaking starship of a once mighty fleet.

I pushed open the door. The moon base–themed interior was looking tired. The Alien Detection scanner at the entrance needed a new bulb, the tentacles poking from air vents lacked their former gooey gleam, and no one had refilled the green Martian gas pumps for weeks. The place smelled stale and was empty save for a couple of customers browsing a dusty display of action figures and someone snoring lightly in a wingback armchair beneath a copy of "The Death of Superman."

At least the shelves were still lined with comics. If anyone would know how to bring about the downfall of Star Guy, it would be Lex Luthor, Magneto, Galactus, or any of the hundreds of other villains who stalked the dark places of the comic book universe. Back in the old days there was something called the Comics Code, which required good to triumph over evil in every issue. And while most stories still followed that pattern, there were examples where the bad guys won, even if the writers had to create alternate universes to let them do so. I gathered a bunch of issues and began my search.

A voice drifted out from behind the cash register propped on the store counter, accompanied by a series of familiar thudding and blasting sound effects. "Ha!

Didn't see that coming, did you? *Fear me!*" Curious, I peered over the high countertop. A skinny sales assistant with a tangle of dark hair sat cross-legged on the floor, playing *Puny Earthlings!* The store stocked a handful of video games and a single console on which to try them. The sales assistant must have swiped it off its stand in the middle of the store in order to play without interruption from bothersome customers.

He studied the screen through a lick of hair that hung down over one eye. "OK, Star Guy," he said, hunching his shoulders and bearing down on the game controller. "Let's see you dodge *this*." He thumbed a complicated sequence of buttons. "Atomic blast! Plasma cannon! Heat ray!" he shouted in quick succession. "Come on, you annoying masked menace—fall out of the sky!" There was a shriek and the sound of tearing metal. I knew what it meant, having experienced it myself each time I played. Star Guy had brought down the Alien Overlord's mother ship.

Game. Over.

"Oh, come on," whined the sales assistant, hurling down the controller. "That's not fair." Star Guy's victory theme song played out over the end credits. I'd heard it so often it had become stuck in my head—the most annoying tune in the universe. As the trumpets blared, the sales assistant noticed my head poking above the counter. He blew the stubborn strand of hair out of his eye. "Can I help you?" he asked, in a tone that made it perfectly clear that he really didn't want to.

What's more, I knew that he *couldn't* help, based on his total failure to put Star Guy out of action. I wouldn't learn any secrets from this guy's feeble game fu. "You've got *Puny Earthlings!* too," I remarked.

"Well, duh," he replied, and grudgingly got to his feet. "Who doesn't?"

"What do you mean?"

"Don't you read GameSpot?"

I hadn't been able to browse the video game site since Mom banned me from unsupervised use of the computer. I shook my head.

He looked at me as if I'd missed the biggest news headline in the world—which I had, if your prime source of news is GameSpot or Kotaku or io9.com. He waved the familiar box that the disc came in. "Two days ago one of these appeared on every doorstep in the area. Our town's been chosen to test the game before it launches worldwide. Are you going to buy those?" He gestured to the comics clutched in my hand.

"No thanks. They're not what I'm looking for."

"Time-waster," he muttered, and sank beneath the counter to continue playing *Puny Earthlings!*

Why had Lab Rat Games given out free copies to

everyone in town? Maybe it was some sort of clever pub-licity campaign. But what mattered was that everyone I knew would be playing the game. Serge, the kids at school who picked on me—all were trying to defeat Star Guy and Dark Flutter. Someone was bound to come up with a solution. I desperately wanted it to be me. Suddenly, it had become a competition.

And why shouldn't I be the one? After all, I had an advantage over the rest of them. Insider knowledge. I knew, for instance, that Zack was mildly allergic to cats, though not enough to knock him out of the sky, not even with some kind of multibarreled, high-velocity, cat-flinging weapon (I'd already built one in the mother ship's R & D lab). But I knew what made him tick. I felt sure that the answer was somewhere in the soup of my relationship with my big brother. If anyone was going to spoon the crouton of his flaw, it would be me.

I headed quickly for the door, itching to get back home to my Xbox and another round with the dratted duo. As I passed the sleeping figure in the armchair, he let out a great snore from beneath the comic propped over his face. The comic slid off and fluttered to the floor. I gasped.

Hidden beneath "The Death of Superman" was a face I never expected to see again.

Christopher Talbot opened one eye.

WE MEET AGAIN

My first instinct was to run. The last time Christopher Talbot and I had been in the same room, he'd sicced his attack robots on me and then tried to shake me off his wildly maneuvering rocket-powered super suit while I clung on for my life.

"You," he rasped, surprise turning into a cough. He looked worn-out. Eyes that once dazzled like gemstones were now dim. Hair that used to be as bouncy as an over-eager Labrador lay limp against his bony skull. Breath rattled through his thin frame. Being struck by a giant asteroid hadn't done him any favors.

During our previous showdown I'd proved that, to his immense annoyance, rather than the hero he believed himself to be, he was in fact a villain. I couldn't imagine he'd forgiven me for that. I gave the store a quick once-over for killer robots. All clear.

He gripped the arms of the chair and with a groan

hauled himself to his feet. "It's good to see you again, Luke," he said, a smile cracking his thin lips. "How have you been?"

"Fine," I said with surprise, and then, drilled by years of my parents telling me always to be polite, I couldn't help adding, "How are you?"

"Oh, you know. After my body was smashed to pieces by the Nemesis asteroid, which I only survived thanks to the protective carapace of my Mark Fourteen Sub-Orbital Super Suit, I woke up in a hospital in South Korea. With amnesia."

I wondered. "Does that mean that you . . . ?"

"'Fraid not. I still remember that your brother is"—he cupped a hand to his mouth and then whispered—"Star Guy."

That was a pity.

He filled me in on the rest of the story. "While I was in the hospital in Seoul, I was put back together by skilled surgeons, but at enormous expense. I had to sell off my business to pay the bills, and then I was shipped home to find, oh great irony, my house a smoking crater, thanks to a stray chunk of asteroid."

"But you had insurance, right?"

"Forgot to renew the policy." He shrugged. "Ah, well, at least I have my health." He dissolved again into a coughing fit. "It really is nice to see you, Luke. Takes me back to the good old days. And a few of the bad. But we'll let that go, shall we?"

Why was he being so friendly? I was highly suspicious. My actions were largely responsible for turning him into this wreck of a man who now stood before me. If I were in his position, I knew what I'd be thinking.

"You're thinking, 'I bet he wants revenge,'" said Christopher Talbot, raising an eyebrow. "You imagine, because of your role in my downfall, I must be plotting to get back at you. Hmm?"

"Well, aren't you?"

He laid a gnarled hand against his cheek and slowly drummed his fingers. "In an ideal world, would I like to take my revenge on Star Guy and his little helpers? Yes. Naturally. Of course I would. Some would say I'd be insane not to. But look at me. I'm penniless and homeless. I sleep in the back room of the store on a futon. You of all people should know that you can't be an effective supervillain without a proper lair and millions to spend on R & D. Death rays don't come cheap. Obviously, they're cheaper than shrink rays, but that's not the point. As for purchasing a suitable property to convert, what with house prices around here—not to mention the city council's planning department—forget it. I mean, really, you build *one* volcano full of radioactive spiders, next thing you know they won't even give you approval for a kitchen extension." He shook his head gloomily.

I wasn't buying it. "So you're saying if only you had the money—and the planning permission—you'd take your revenge?"

"I'm not saying that at all. You forget, I never intended to be the villain. I wanted to be the hero." He looked past me with a faraway expression. "My whole life, all I dreamed of was becoming a superhero." He blinked. "But that's over. The man you see before you is no more than a humble comic book seller."

I didn't believe a word. I searched his face for a clue to his real intentions, but all I could see were wrinkles. "What about your close call with Nemesis?"

"What about it?"

Did he take me for a complete fool? "You want me to believe you got that close to the biggest asteroid in the galaxy and it *didn't* give you superpowers?"

He nodded. "Fair point. Gaining superpowers from an asteroid or meteorite is a classic, some might even argue overused, comic device. Indeed, it is a route I myself have pursued, in my less enlightened past." He thought for a moment. "Well, I do get a tingling sensation in my right foot now when the weather's about to change, but I think that might be due to a touch of arthritis." He placed one hand over his heart and threw out the other, then said in a weird, trembly voice:

"Now my charms are all o'erthrown,
and what strength I have's mine own,
which is most faint."

He looked at me. "*The Tempest*," he explained.

"From *Ultimate X-Men?*"

He sighed. "From Shakespeare."

Nope. I still didn't believe him. I'd seen it too many times. The villain defeated in one story comes back in the next, and this time he's seen the error of his ways and he's all goody-goody. But it's a trick! And just when the hero least expects it, he reveals his true evil face and—

"I know what you're thinking."

"Aha!" I jumped on his admission. "Because you have telepathy."

"No, Luke, because we're alike. We could have been friends." He gave an awkward cough. "If I hadn't tried to destroy your brother and knock you off my super suit. Anyway, bygones and all that. And you're wrong. I'm not pretending to be innocent while plotting some evil payback. I'm done. Finished. Out of the supervillain business."

He had to be lying.

"I'm not lying."

"Swear on it."

"OK. Yes. If that'll help you believe me. So, what shall

I swear on?" He shambled over to a shelf of comic books and plucked one down. "How about Doctor Strange's magic order? *By the Hoary Hosts of Hoggoth* . . . No? Ah, now here's a classic. He-Man's proclamation. *By the power of Grayskull . . . I have the power.* But no Power Sword, so that doesn't work. Wait, I know. Oh, this is perfect. I'll swear on the oath of the Green Lantern Corps."

"No," I said firmly.

"The *Blue* Lantern Corps? OK. Niche. But OK."

I had a much better idea. "Swear you're not a super-villain . . . on Star Guy's oath."

Serge had come up with the oath, and like everything else to do with Star Guy, after Nemesis its popularity had exploded. I said he should claim royalties, but Serge said that wouldn't be in the right spirit. Then Q-Piddy used it as the lyrics for his song "Stop Me Before I Chill Again" and bought an island with the profits.

The important thing was that the oath would help me determine once and for all if Christopher Talbot was telling the truth. I knew it was cruel to force him to say the oath of the superhero who had defeated him, but if the words stuck in his throat, then I'd have my answer.

Christopher Talbot swallowed. A bead of sweat, a nervous twitch—I was looking for the smallest sign. He began to recite the words.

"Granted cosmic superpower
In our darkest hour,
Star Guy, star light,
Protector of the world tonight."

"There," he said, clapping his hands. "Now, how about a nice cup of tea? I have cookies."

"What kind?"

"Poisoned," he said, and waggled his eyebrows.

I knew he was joking but decided not to eat them anyway.

"Would you mind?" He gestured to a cane propped against the back of the chair.

I gave it to him. He leaned on the stick and began to limp off. As he passed the counter he saw that no one was manning the store.

"Rafe," he called out. I guessed he was looking for the sales assistant with the stubborn bangs. "Rafe Peacock, where are you?!" He tutted. "I can't even afford proper help these days. He's my sister's boy. I was doing her a favor." He pointed the cane at the abandoned cash register. "Now, nepotism, there's a terrible power."

I'd never heard of nepotism, but it was weird to think of Christopher Talbot having a family. You don't read much about villains' family life in comics. I wondered why. Maybe it would make them too sympathetic, knowing that they had a mom and dad.

"It's Rafe's last day working here. When he's gone, it'll just be me. Ah, well." He looked around the empty store. "Now, where were we? Yes. Tea and cookies."

I caught myself. Afternoon tea with the villain formerly known as the Quintessence—what was I thinking? "I'm sorry, I have to go," I said quickly, and hurried for the door.

His face fell. "Yes, yes. Of course. I understand."

I glanced back. Christopher Talbot stood hunched over his cane. "Another time then." He smiled sadly and shuffled off toward his little room at the back of the store.

I stumbled onto the pavement and took a deep lungful of air. I hadn't realized that I'd been holding my breath for so long. I had the oddest sensation. It took me a few moments to pin it down. As impossible as it seemed, I felt sorry for Christopher Talbot.

BOTTOM OF THE BAG

I wandered Main Street, my head whirling after my strange encounter. Christopher Talbot was alive. He must be up to something. Or had he hung up his mask and cape, as he claimed? He'd passed my Star Guy oath stress test, which was pretty conclusive. But even the toughest test could be outwitted. Hadn't Captain Kirk outsmarted the unwinnable Kobayashi Maru? Hadn't Parminder Chaudry scored a perfect 100 percent in the unbeatable mental arithmetic (non-calculator) test?

Zack had accused me of seeing supervillains everywhere. Was this another of those times? Christopher Talbot *had* been a supervillain, but only by accident—or so he said. I was confused. Usually I trusted my instincts, but I'd gotten it spectacularly wrong with Miss Dunham, and somewhere between the kids at school and my brother, I'd lost my confidence. What I needed was a second opinion. I took the bus out of the town center and headed for Serge's house.

Serge lived in a *cul-de-sac*, which is French. Perhaps his parents chose it because it reminded them of home. Two bicycles lay in the driveway. I recognized Serge's Peugeot mountain bike, but there was also a sleek racer that I hadn't seen before, with upgraded Shimano pedals and carbon-rimmed wheels.

I couldn't ring the doorbell, in case his *maman* was home, so I snuck around the back. Serge's bedroom overlooked a small yard with a statue of a winged boy that peed into a round pond. When we first met, we'd figured out that his bedroom window faced mine, and we'd spent a week and a half, each standing in our own house, waving and shining increasingly bright lights to establish if we could see one another. We could not. There was no direct line of sight, and we were separated by 2.3 miles of suburb.

I cupped my hands to my mouth and hooted like an owl. It wasn't a prearranged signal or anything; it just felt like the right thing to do. After a few more hoots, Serge appeared. He unlatched the window and threw it open.

"Ah, I thought it must be you," he said in a low voice. "What are you doing here?"

I was about to reply when another figure joined him at the window. I could barely believe my eyes. It was Josh Khan. The grinning architect of my misery. With my best friend.

"Well, if it isn't Luke Pie-walker himself." Josh cackled.

"That isn't funny," I said. "It doesn't even make sense."

"Of course it's funny," he said with a snarl. "Steve, tell him it's funny."

Steve? Who was he calling Steve?

Serge looked from Josh to me and back again. "Ah, I would not like to say. I often struggle with your clever English wordplay. A lot of it does not translate, you know."

I could see that Josh didn't care. "Whatever. I've got better things to do than waste my time talking to a loser like Cry-walker here. *Cry-walker.* Now that is funny. Come on, Steve." He disappeared back into the room. Serge lingered at the window.

"Steve?" I said.

Serge grimaced. "He was not listening properly when we were introduced, and it has gone on so long now that it would be impolite to correct him. And possibly hazardous."

I couldn't get my head around what had happened. "When did you two even become friends?"

"Our *mamans* put us together. They believed it would be a good idea. His family once spent a week at a *gîte* in Brittany." He shrugged. "I have been stuck playing *Puny Earthlings!* with him since the commencement of the break."

Serge had teamed up with my worst enemy to play the game I so desperately wanted to win. "Have you defeated Star Guy yet?" I asked, holding my breath as I awaited the answer.

"*Non,*" said Serge. "It is that force field of his. It protects both him and Dark Flutter, and it is impenetrable."

Good. Victory was still up for grabs. At least that was something. I was about to tell him about Christopher Talbot when I heard the rattle of a car engine in the driveway.

"It is my *maman,*" cried Serge. "She has returned from Zumba."

"Where's Zumba?"

"It is not a where; it is a what. But that is not important right now. You must disappear, *immédiatement.*"

"Don't worry, I'm like Batman," I said. "Silent, undetectable, invisi—"

"Luke."

"OK, OK, I'm going." I paused. "But I need to talk to you about something important. Meet me in the tree house tonight."

"I cannot. You know that."

"Serge, listen to me. Christopher Talbot is alive. And I think he's plotting a comeback. Anyway, I need you."

In the silence that followed, the only sound was water whizzing from the statue of the winged boy.

"STEVE!" Josh's voice boomed. "I'M WAITING!"

"I am sorry," said Serge. And before I could object, he tugged the window shut and was gone.

WITH GREAT POWER COMES GREAT ANNOYANCE

I trudged home with a heavy heart. How could Serge do this to me? What had the world come to, when he'd rather hang out with Josh Khan than join me in the tree house to hatch an overly complicated plan to thwart a potential supervillain?

If he wasn't going to help, then perhaps another member of the old gang would. A little over half an hour later, I found myself on Lara's doorstep. Her big sister (and the object of Zack's affection), Cara, opened the door.

Cara was fourteen and dangerous. Not the "poisonous bite" or "razor-sharp claws" kind of danger, but the kind that takes a long look at the world and says, "Out of my way—I'm coming through." She had sleek black hair and blue fingernails. She wore a glittering nose stud, and there was a rumor she'd gone by herself to a music festival in a field. She was as tall as Finn Stanton, captain of the school football team, and she had a Viking boyfriend called Matthias, who'd once met someone who'd seen Nebula from *Guardians of the Galaxy* in a Walgreens.

She tugged out her earbuds. I got a blast of the new Billy Dark album. "Hey, kid." Cara had a low-slung voice, and her words seemed to slide out as if they'd been slouching on beanbags, waiting for a shove. She called me *kid* these days. I think it was because she couldn't remember my name, but I kind of liked it anyway.

"Hi, Cara. Is Lara in?"

"Yeah. For a change." She shook her head. "I've never known anyone who spent as much time at the library as my sis. She's turned into a serious bookworm."

So Lara was using the same cover story as Zack, pretending to be studying when she was in fact out performing heroic feats, faster than a speeding squirrel.

"Yeah, I know what you mean," I said. "My brother's at the library all the time. In fact, he's there *so* often I'd call him a book-*sand*worm. That's a really huge kind of worm. From Arrakis, the desert planet, source of the spice melange. Actually, they're more like a lamprey than a—"

"She's in her room," Cara said abruptly, standing aside to let me past.

I trotted upstairs to Lara's bedroom and was raising my fist to knock when the door flew open. She stood there clutching a gym bag, which I knew contained her Dark Flutter costume.

"Luke, hi. I'm really sorry, but I'm just going out." She patted the gym bag. "Is it a bird? Is it a plane? No, it's *me*." She smiled. "You know how it is." She swept past me to the top of the stairs. "Off to the library," she said in a loud voice for the benefit of her big sister. Cara was below in the hall, smooching with her boyfriend, Matthias the Viking, in front of a coatrack.

"Can it wait a minute?" I said in an urgent whisper. "This is important."

She hesitated. "Let me check." With that, she closed her eyes.

I knew instantly what was going on: she was communicating telepathically with Zack. I felt a prickle of envy.

"Zack says I can have five minutes."

"That's nice of him," I said tightly. "I didn't know you'd started doing that together."

"Telepathic communication? Oh, yes. Why bother with phones or squirrels when you can just think to each other, right?"

"Right."

"And maybe once we've discussed your important business," said Lara with a nervous smile, "I can tell you about mine? I really need to talk to you, Luke. Only you."

"Sure." I glanced down at the canoodling couple,

concerned that they might overhear our conversation. "Perhaps we should continue this in private?" I turned to her bedroom. The door was ajar.

"Uh, no, you can't go in there." She threw herself between me and the door.

"Why not?" I squinted past her through the gap. Her room looked remarkably spick-and-span. I had a suspicion that was immediately confirmed by the flash of a bobbed tail. "Are you using woodland creatures to tidy your room?"

"No."

"Lara?"

"OK, OK. So maybe. Please don't tell Zack. He says using your powers for anything other than heroic acts is a slippery slope to the dark side."

I fumed. *He* hadn't said that; *I* had.

There was a squeak at our feet. A gray rabbit crouched in the doorway.

"No, the red top can go in the dresser drawer," said Lara. The rabbit hopped back into the bedroom. "Now, what was it you had to tell me?"

I filled her in on my encounter with Christopher Talbot. When I'd finished, she thought for a moment and then said, "You should tell Zack. It sounds important, and I'm sure he'll be right on it." She touched my arm. "Luke, I'm glad you came. We really haven't had a chance to talk in ages. So much has happened." She paused. "Y'know, it's funny, but at first when Zorbon gave me my superpower, I was frightened. I didn't know what to do. I wasn't even sure I wanted to be a superhero. But then Zack said something that helped me understand. *Not everyone is meant to make a difference, but for me the choice to lead an ordinary life is no longer an option.* Isn't that amazing? Your brother is so wise."

I couldn't believe what I was hearing. "It was Spider-Man," I spluttered. "*Spider-Man* said that. Not *Zack.*"

"Well, anyway, Zack was wise to repeat it." Lara's eyes shone. "And now I love being Dark Flutter. When I'm older I'm going to be a vet during the day and Dark Flutter the rest of the time. I'll be able to ask a Labrador where it hurts, show a swan the right exercises for that broken wing. I can't wait for the rest of my life to begin. Can you?"

"*Can't wait,*" I mumbled. To me the thought of growing up was filled with anxieties about school, girls, and melting polar ice caps. Mostly the future felt like a big, scary secret that no one would let me in on. It was all right for Lara and Zack—they had a purpose, a shield to protect them against the unknown. Me? I was defenseless and completely clueless.

"But there is one thing . . ." began Lara. She cleared her throat awkwardly. "I don't know quite how to say this. You and I have been through a lot together. You're like my—oh, hang on."

Zack was calling again, asking for an ETA. Our time had come to an end. Lara had to fly.

"Mustn't fiddle while foam burns," she said.

"Rome," I said with a sigh. "It's while *Rome* burns."

She shot me a puzzled look. "It's a fire in a mattress factory."

I left her so she could go be super-heroic, and walked the short distance home, feeling wretched. She hadn't finished her sentence. "You're like my—" What? Dorky neighbor? Weirdo friend? As I hung up my coat in the hallway, unkind thoughts swirled in my head. She was so full of herself, but really, what a ridiculous super-power. The ability to talk to hedgehogs—ooh, how amazing. And listening to her *go on* about Zack, how he's so understanding and *wise*. Resentment boiled over like a forgotten pot of spaghetti. There was only one thing to do: I needed to play *Puny Earthlings!* and blast them both out of the sky. Right now.

In the living room, my dad was Skyping his dad in Scotland. When I was little, my grandparents wanted to see me a lot, so every afternoon I'd be propped in front of an iPad while they made goo-goo noises and pulled faces. For years I thought they were an app.

My dad still talked to his dad when he needed advice.

They were discussing Dad's job situation. I knew he'd applied for a new one but hadn't heard anything back yet, which meant he'd be at home the whole week. Usually, old Mrs. Wilson from next door looked after us during vacations. She's deaf in one ear, only wears slippers, and has the vision of a mole. In other words, the perfect sitter. But based on yesterday's epic gaming session, Dad was going to be much more fun.

"There's my favorite grandson!" bellowed Grandpa Bernard from the screen as I entered the camera's field of view.

"Dad," said my dad. "You can't have favorites."

I didn't care. I was glad to be someone's favorite.

"Uh, I know that," said Grandpa. "But look at the boy." He beamed. "So how's life with you, Zack?"

Zack? *Zack?!* Even *he* preferred my big brother.

Dad told Grandpa Bernard to adjust his glasses, and after that he mumbled an apology. We chatted for a while. He and Grandma were coming to visit soon for my cousin Jenny's wedding. The reception was going to be held at the golf club, and I had to wear a suit and pinchy shoes. There was no getting out of it. It was the Van Kull Maximum Security Facility of weddings.

We said good-bye and put down the iPad. "How about a game of *Puny Earthlings!?*" I suggested to Dad.

"Ah," he said.

That didn't sound good. Concerned, I glanced under the TV. Instead of my Xbox there was now a console-shaped hole. "Where is it?"

"Ah," repeated Dad. "You know how your mother never suspected a thing about our gaming session yesterday?"

My face fell. "Oh no . . ." She knew. She *always* knew. This was awful. "When did she say I could have it back?"

Dad squirmed. "You can't."

"Where is it? Where did you put it? In the hall cupboard? Your room?"

"On eBay."

"No! You can't. It's mine. I—" I felt hot tears prick my eyes. This was so unfair.

"Luke, son, it's not Mom's fault; it's mine. I shouldn't have let you play with it. But I was feeling sorry for myself and . . . I'm not sure if video games are actually dangerous, but I do know that they're a real time-suck. I lost some of the best years of my life to something called *Half-Life*." He looked dazed. "One minute I'm battling Vortigaunts at Black Mesa, and the next thing I know I'm picking tableware with your mother for our wedding registry."

I was too angry to hear him. All I knew was that he was selling my Xbox. "Is this because you need the money now that you're unemployed?" It was a cruel thing to say, and I regretted it immediately.

Dad's face crumpled. He looked like he'd been struck by a super-aging ray. I tried to say sorry, but the words stuck in my throat. I fled to my room.

I slammed the door and flung myself onto my bed, fuming at the injustice of the world. All of the people I trusted had let me down. No one in my life understood me or had any idea what I was going through. I rolled onto my back and stared at the ceiling. The ticking of my Green Arrow alarm clock filled the silence. Although that wasn't entirely true.

There was one person.

THE WRATH OF LUKE

"You want a what?" asked Christopher Talbot.

It was nine thirty the following morning, and I was standing on the doorstep of Crystal Comics. I'd been hammering to get in since nine, which, according to the sign, was when it was supposed to open.

"A Job," I repeated.

He peered down at me with a wary expression. "If this was Victorian England and I had a blocked chimney, well then, a short, wiry boy like yourself? I'd hire you in a flash. But you're what—six? Seven?"

"Eleven," I said through gritted teeth.

"Eleven. Really? Makes no difference. There are things called employment laws. Good-bye." He pushed the door shut.

I shoved a foot in the narrowing gap. "Uh, you launched a rocket-powered super suit from a volcano in the middle of town and used a superpower-sucking machine on my brother, so don't tell me you care about laws."

Christopher Talbot pursed his thin lips in displeasure. I sensed he was wavering. "And what's more, according to that"—I pointed to the sign—"this place should have been open long before now. Your nephew quit. You don't have anyone else. You need me."

His face was a mask. Not a supervillain mask—the other kind, that doesn't give anything away. But I knew he was thinking seriously about what I'd said. I decided to sweeten the deal. "You wouldn't even have to pay me," I added. "So technically I wouldn't be employed, which means you wouldn't be breaking any laws."

I had to get this job. I needed it more than I'd ever thought possible.

"I know that look," said Christopher Talbot, fixing me with his TARDIS-blue eyes. "Seen it in the mirror a hundred times. You're plotting something."

"You've found me out," I said, holding up my hands in mock surrender. I leaned toward him and whispered, "I want to take over the world."

He was suitably startled. Taking advantage of his surprise, I pushed past him into the store. He stood in the open doorway, tracking me like an automatic sentry gun. "This is some kind of trick, isn't it?" He stabbed a finger at my Deadpool backpack. "You've got some sort of surveillance device in there, don't you? This is entrapment, that's what it is. Not that I'm planning anything villainous. *Whatsoever.* Got that, whoever's listening to this?" He glanced out onto busy Main Street, scanning the passersby. "That annoying brother of yours sent you, didn't he?"

"My annoying brother has nothing to do with me being here," I said. "Well, he does, but not in the way you mean." I'd found what I came for. Dumped on a shelf behind the counter was the chunky, oh-so-touchable shape of a video game console.

I gazed into the black depths of the precision-molded plastic and saw my own face staring back. At least it looked like me, but I could swear there was something about the face gazing back that was different. Something fluttered behind my reflection's head. It seemed to be . . . a cape. Had to be some trick of the light. Before I could look again, another face swam out of the gloom. Christopher Talbot stood at my shoulder, enveloping me in a cloud of minty toothpaste and salami sandwich breath.

"Can't stand these things," he said, gesturing to the console. "Wouldn't even have one in the store, except your generation can't get enough of them. Video games." He shook his head with displeasure. "Whatever happened to a good old-fashioned game of Red Rover?" He had a misty look in his eye. "Two dozen taunting schoolkids trying to drag down a small child on a concrete playground." He sighed. "All right then."

"All right what?" I asked uncertainly.

"You've got the job," he said. "No overtime, no 401(k), and you have to provide your own sandwiches."

"I already brought them," I said, indicating my backpack.

"Course you did. Right. I'm off for a nap." He threw a salute. "Commander, the bridge is yours." With that he leaned on his cane and hobbled off toward the back of the store.

As soon as I heard the soft thud of his door shutting, I locked the front door and turned the sign to Closed. I didn't want to be disturbed (and it wasn't as if people were lining up to get in). I hurried over to the counter, removed the Xbox from its shelf, set it up in front of the screen, and reached for the game disc. The overhead lights shone through its layers to reveal a gorgeous spiderweb of circuitry under the surface. I'd never seen anything like it. Lab Rat Games must have spent a fortune on the design. I slotted the disc into the machine, and as I waited for the game to load, I unzipped my backpack. In addition to my sandwiches, I'd brought a pair of headphones. The console whirred to life, and I felt myself relax. I slipped on the headphones, and the outside world faded away. This was what I needed. The sure touch of the controller, the instant feedback, the pinpoint control I had over my alien fleet. This is what I could rely on—not Serge, not Lara, not Mom or Dad, and especially not my big brother. As I played I sensed I was not alone. All across town, hundreds, perhaps thousands, of people were doing the same thing, focused on blasting the dratted Star Guy and his annoying sidekick out of the sky.

But how to conquer Earth's last line of defense?

I ran through precisely what I was up against. Star Guy could fly, breathe in outer space; he had the powers of telekinesis and telepathy, a Star Screen radar, and a force field. He needed starlight to power up, but he could go for days without needing to recharge. And Dark Flutter had . . . pigeons. She wasn't a threat. No, *he* was the obstacle.

My mother ship went down in flames. Star Guy's victory theme blared in my headphones. No matter. I had time. All day, in fact. Mom was at work, and Dad thought I was at Serge's house. Dad had barely noticed when I slipped out that morning, and he hadn't questioned my cover story. He was too busy watching endless YouTube clips of old TV shows from his childhood. He does this when he's feeling old and sad. When Dad got like this he was not easily distracted.

I restarted the game from the last checkpoint.

Not easily distracted. An idea tickled the back of my

brain. Perhaps Zack's greatest power was not one that Zorbon had given him. I thought it through. Zack could sit in the library and study for hours and hours. Not only could he leap tall buildings in a single bound, he could also read a math textbook from cover to cover without moving a muscle. Forget about telekinesis and Star Screens; his greatest powers were his powers of concentration. The tickle became an itch. I felt the stirrings of an actual plan. I'd studied him in the heat of battle; I knew that he had to concentrate in order to use his powers. The solution to my problem rose up like a fin in the water.

Break his concentration and you break Star Guy.

Unable to focus, he would drop his force field, and without it he'd be vulnerable to a blast directed from my mother ship's weapon systems. I did a quick calculation. My alien-targeting computers were lightning fast, so it would take just two seconds to lock on and fire. Two seconds without his protective shield, and victory would be mine.

One part of the puzzle remained. How to distract him? What I needed was a tactical shepherd's pie. Not an actual shepherd's pie, but something that would work the same way on Zack.

I was so close. I could feel the answer just beyond my fingertips. But just as I reached for it, there was a dull knocking in my headphones. I slipped them off and the knocking grew louder. Someone was at the front door. Grumbling, I paused the game. I opened the door to a motorbike courier delivering a package for Christopher Talbot.

"Ine ear id," said the courier.

"Pardon me?"

The courier removed her helmet. Long hair spilled over leather-jacketed shoulders. She peeled off a glove, and as she thrust the handheld signing device at me and tapped a stylus against the screen, I noticed her finger-nails were painted blue. "Sign here, kid," she repeated.

I was frozen to the spot.

"You OK?" asked the courier.

The answer to the puzzle was standing in front of me (in a manner of speaking). I signed for the package and rushed back to the game. I didn't have to distract Star Guy; I had to distract *Zack*. Swiftly, I navigated to the Overlord menu, accessed the R & D laboratory, selected the nanomachine replicator, and set to work designing the device that I knew would stop him in his tracks. I labored for minutes. And then it was done. The very last part of the process was to give the weapon a suitably awesome name. I thought for a moment and then began to enter my choice, using the controller. I meant to call it the "Doomsday Machine," but I made a typo, and seeing as it took ages to select the letters, I didn't bother to go back to fix it. So it ended up being called the "Doofsday Machine."

I restarted the game. My device primed, I launched another invasion of Earth. I swept aside the tanks and planes as usual, and waited. Two streaks appeared on the horizon: Star Guy and Dark Flutter were coming. But this time I was ready for them.

I gently pressed the FIRE button and unleashed my secret weapon. It worked just as I'd planned. The force field flickered and dropped. Two seconds later my weapon systems boomed, and I was rewarded with the glorious sight of Star Guy and Dark Flutter tumbling out of the sky to their doom.

I leaped to my feet and punched the air. I'd done it— crushed them both! My victory cry lodged in my throat. A high-pitched whine was rising from the console. I barely had time to turn my head toward it before a flash of green light exploded from the machine, and my world went dark.

A BIG TENTACLE FOR OUR
WINNER

I opened my eyes and winced as a sliver of light poked me like a bony finger.

"The Thucwex Gsuphlon has arrived," boomed a voice that seemed to come from everywhere. There was a sound like someone clapping wet hands. "Bring the nourishment."

As my vision adjusted, I began to make out my surroundings. I was lying on some kind of raised platform in the center of a large, rectangular room with two doors. A single column of light shone down on me from the ceiling far above. Markings crisscrossed the floor, multicolored straight lines and curves I felt sure I'd seen somewhere before. A movement caught my eye. High up one wall was a viewing window, behind which huddled shadowy figures, observing me. I felt like a specimen on a microscope slide. I sat up. My head throbbed, and I had an overwhelming desire for—

"Grilled cheese, oh great and terrible Thucwex?"

There was a faint buzzing next to my ear. I turned to find some kind of hovering drone with a bulbous electronic eye that swiveled at the end of a stalk. The weird thing was that the drone looked familiar. It held out a silver plate on which lay a slice of toast with a slab of melted white cheese.

"Halloumi," said the voice. "Not only the squeakiest cheese in the universe, but one of the saltiest. Your biology requires such replenishment after your journey."

Journey? What was the voice talking about? I examined the grilled cheese greedily. It might have been poisoned, but I didn't care. I wolfed it down, and slipped off the podium. "Where am I? Who are you?" I addressed the figures behind the high window.

"One question at a time," said the voice. "Lower the blast shields," it commanded.

With a rumble, a section of wall parted, leaving an unobstructed view out. I'd seen this view a hundred times, but only in photos with a NASA logo in one corner.

Before me lay the spinning green and blue marble of planet Earth.

"We are in geostationary orbit above the oblate ellipsoid known to you as Earth," explained the voice calmly. "In your standard measure, twenty-three thousand miles above coordinates fifty-one degrees, twenty-two minutes, thirty-nine-point-nine seconds latitude; zero degrees, two minutes, thirty-six-point-five-one seconds longitude. Or, as I am sure you have already calculated, directly above Route 95 at the corner of Brewery Road."

Suddenly, I remembered where I had seen the drone before. "I'm on the mother ship from *Puny Earthlings!*" I breathed.

"Such insight, such reckoning," said the voice, impressed. "Truly he is the Thucwex Gsuphlon."

"A new season brings a new Thucwex," chanted more voices.

I reeled about the room in shock, legs wobbling beneath me. I stumbled and threw out a hand to steady myself. It brushed against a rope hanging from the ceiling. Curious. The jumble of thoughts in my head arranged themselves in some sort of order. The green flash from the Xbox just after I'd defeated Star Guy in the game must have been a teleportation beam. I'd been *beamed up.* And yet this place didn't look like any transporter room I'd seen in comics or on TV. Where were the beaming bays? The control panels with dozens of sliders? I pushed the questions from my mind—I had other things to worry about. If this was the mother ship, then the shadowy figures in the viewing window were aliens.

Actual extraterrestrials. And if they were anything like the ones in the video game, they didn't come in peace.

"I know you're planning to take over the world," I said. "But you won't succeed."

"Yes, we thought so too," said the voice smugly. "Until you came along, oh dreadful Thucwex."

"What are you talking about? And why do you keep calling me that? What's a Thucwex?"

"How shall I explain?" There was a sound I can only describe as a polite cough into a clenched tentacle. "Who knows the earthlings better than themselves? Who better to plot their downfall than one of their own? That video game you are so obsessed with? The key to our plan. It was the maze and you the laboratory rats. In your language, we 'crowdsourced' our invasion plan."

The game. The game was a trick.

The voice let out a laugh at its own cleverness, one that sounded like a mouthful of slapping tongues.

"The only obstacle to our inevitable conquest has been the one known as Star Guy," the smug alien went on. "For some time now we have been testing his abilities, probing him for a weakness. For example, unnoticed by your planet's laughable military forces, we used our mighty electromagnetic pulse weapon to bring down three of your atmospheric craft."

The airplanes. I knew it!

"Star Guy proved to be up to the challenge. As he did with the threat from our genetically modified grocery clerk and the evil artificial intelligence we planted in JCPenney."

This was all part of the aliens' master plan. Such cunning.

"Star Guy is a formidable foe," declared the voice.

Typical. Even the aliens were impressed by my annoying brother.

"Indeed, for a time we considered him too formidable. But then we found you. We computed that the citizens of the realm where Star Guy resides would know him better than anyone else on the planet. They would understand his failings, help us target his vulnerabilities. And here you are. Thanks to your highly inventive solution, now we know how to crush him. You are the Thucwex Gsuphlon," rasped the voice. "The Bringer of Ruin."

"A new season brings a new Thucwex," chanted the others.

Horrified, I leaned back against the wall and slid to the floor. For years I'd dreamed of being the Chosen One, but not like this. I'd shown the aliens how to defeat Star Guy. I was the villain. I was the end of the world.

"And now we shall reveal ourselves," intoned the voice.

Head in my hands, I was vaguely aware of the relentless march of approaching feet.

"We have scanned your brain. Based on the image search of your tiny mind, we shall present ourselves in a form designed to strike fear into your meager cardiovascular system. *One* heart? Pathetic weakling race."

I was less concerned with the insult than with the idea of facing my worst fear. "*What?* Why would you do that?"

"One must give the audience what they want," said the voice.

What did that mean? I cringed at the thought of what slimy, multiheaded, slavering nastiness they'd dredged up from my vivid imagination.

A high-pitched shriek rose above the beat of marching feet, and another and another, until the jangling sound drove out every thought from my spinning head. Whatever horrifying form the aliens had taken, they were about to come through the door.

The first shadow fell across the threshold; then quickly one, two, three figures jogged through the doorway, all wearing light-blue tracksuits and blowing Acme Thunderer silver-plated whistles.

A seemingly endless line of Miss Dunhams trotted into the room.

By the time all of them had arrived, I was ringed by hundreds of duplicate gym teachers, whistles screeching, jogging on the spot. Only then, looking around me, did I see that the podium I had woken up on was a pommel horse, the rope I'd brushed against was a massive climbing rope, and the crisscross markings on the floor outlined a variety of sports courts.

The aliens' transporter room was a near-perfect replica of the school gym.

One Miss Dunham emerged from the pack and, placing her hands on her hips, addressed me over the terrible clamor. Though she looked like all the rest, I was sure this was the alien I'd been talking to. That familiar cruel smile spread across her lips.

"Luke Parker. Well, well, well." She sounded just like the real Miss Dunham. "Our name is unpronounceable in your whiny, ridiculous language." She turned to the others. "Only *one* tongue." The others whistled their amusement. The leader took a step toward me, and I shrank back. "So you may call us . . . the *sue-dunham*. Know then that I am the Supreme Intergalactic Overlord and, thanks to you, soon-to-be ruler of Earth."

Not if I could help it. If I could discover the aliens' reasons for invading, I might be able to figure out a way to defeat them. Aliens always had ridiculous reasons for invading Earth. And usually they hadn't done enough advance planning about the bugs in our atmosphere, or they hadn't updated the virus software on their mother ship. In comics and films they were always being thwarted.

"Have you run out of water?" I asked.

"What?" snapped the Overlord.

"Is that why you're invading us? To steal Earth's water?"

"Our oceans are vast, our weather cycle in perfect harmony. We have no need of your pitiful H_2O."

"Then you're here for food."

"Food?"

"Yes, some natural disaster on your planet means you can no longer feed your own people, so you're going to harvest us and turn us into human-being burgers."

"That's . . . disgusting. And highly caloric. No."

"OK, OK. Then you're afraid of us and this is an early strike to make sure we never become a threat."

"No." She sounded bored now.

"You want our gold?"

"Nope."

"DNA?"

"Uh-uh."

"Millions of years ago you visited Earth and seeded the human race, and now you've come back in order to—"

She raised a hand. "I'm going to stop you there." She took a step toward me. "I know what you're up to—I've met individuals like you before. And let me assure you, we have prepared for *every* eventuality. We do this *a lot*. And if you think I'm going to stand here and divulge our plans, then"—she smiled thinly—"you're quite right."

13

THE DOOFSDAY MACHINE

The Overlord swung one hand up from her hip, clutching what at first I took to be a weapon. I winced as she leveled the device at me, and then relaxed when I saw that it looked remarkably like a TV remote control. She thumbed a large green button. In any language—even an alien one—it had to be the ON switch.

There was a buzz and a shimmer as a giant screen materialized out of nowhere. It floated inches from my face, weightless and glowing. An image of a spinning planet appeared.

"Behold our home world," she began. "A peaceful planet: a climate in perfect balance, a contented population." The picture changed to a flyover of rolling green countryside and thick, forested hillsides, giving way to vast deserts, soaring mountain ranges, and deep blue oceans. "For thousands of years we existed with no hunger, no sickness, no need of money, no need to work. To be honest, it was getting kind of boring."

The picture changed again, this time displaying clips of what I took to be TV shows. From what I could tell of the rapidly changing imagery, there was a sitcom starring a family of robots, another about a talking dog doctor, a drama set in a big country house with squids in gowns, a game show where you could win a fridge with arms, and lots of alien police shows.

"To amuse our people, our TV channels evolved to a level of entertainment unmatched in the history of the universe—except perhaps for five years of the cable channel you call HBO. We created the funniest comedies, the most moving dramas, until finally we reached the acknowledged pinnacle of TV entertainment: *reality shows.* But our audience craved more. More excitement. More teary moments. More explosions. And so there was just one logical development."

The screen filled with the hulking shape of a spaceship. Its hull bristled with alien gun platforms, missile tubes, and the biggest satellite dish I'd ever set eyes on. The Overlord turned to me. "We weaponized our entertainment." She smiled. "Thus we created the reality TV show to end all shows. It has everything: drama, comedy, cliff-hangers, guest stars, exotic locations, giant robots, unexpected twists, and lots—*and lots*—of explosions. The concept is simple—all the best ones are. Each season, we travel to a far-off star system and invade a new planet." She leaned in. "And this year, it's yours."

My brain tried to process what I had just heard and could only spit out a great big "Huh?" Surely she wasn't saying that the invasion of Earth was a reality show?

"You'll never get away with it," I squeaked.

"Are you kidding?" sneered the Overlord. "We *always* win. *The Show* has been running continuously for a thousand years. It is more than entertainment; it is our way of life—as it will become yours."

I felt a bead of sweat roll down my back. "What do you mean?"

The Overlord clicked her remote control again. An image of a classroom appeared, filled with sue-dunham wearing headsets and sitting in front of more of those floating displays. It looked like one of our ICT classrooms. ICT stood for "Information and Communications Technology," although maybe that should have been renamed "Invasion Command and Transmission." "Once we conquer your world, you and every other earthling will be hooked up to our interplanetary broadcasting network, allowing us to beam *The Show* directly into your brain, blocking out everything else—*for the rest of your life*. Soon, like billions before you, all you will care about is *The Show*." She paused. "Think of it not as an invasion but more like a connection fee." She turned to address the sue-dunham horde, intoning, "The audience must grow."

They chanted their response. "The audience must grow."

And as the chilling sound faded, the Overlord commanded in a loud, braying voice, "Activate the Doofsday Machine."

I was aware of a surge of activity among the crew as they hurried to carry out her order.

"Our finest military minds were tasked with devising a plan to defeat Star Guy," said the Overlord, with a fierce glance toward a line of aliens at the front of the sue-dunham ranks. "All failed." The aliens hung their heads. "But where they disappointed me, you, Luke Parker of Earth, have triumphed!"

There was a ripple of movement at the door to the girls' locker room as the alien invaders made way for a new arrival.

"While my generals thought like soldiers, you were not bound by their plodding predictability," she continued. "Yes, somehow even with just one slow, insufficient brain, you took an imaginative leap. And like all the great solutions—the gravimatic wave refractor, the solar-density ramscoop, the infrared TV remote—yours was so simple. You could not defeat the superhero, so you did not try. No, your evil brilliance was to target the weakling human being behind the mask. Behold!" The Overlord signaled to the crowd, who, with a squeak of sneakers against the metal deck, promptly stood aside to allow a familiar figure to pass.

Cara Lee strolled into the center of the room.

"Hi, kid," she drawled.

It looked like her. Spoke like her. Except I knew it wasn't her. If the aliens had followed my plan to the letter, then the thing that stood before me was in fact—

"A perfect robot replica." The Overlord slowly circled the look-alike Cara, admiring her from every angle. "Forged in the nano laboratories of this very mother ship, she is a flawless copy of the young human female known to you as Cara Marjorie Lee."

Marjorie? She'd kept that quiet.

The Overlord was right: the robot was uncannily lifelike. If I didn't know better, I'd be fooled, which was the whole point of the plan. *My* plan, I remembered with a gulp.

"What better way to distract a teenage boy superhero than with a teenage girl?" The Overlord pushed her face into the Cara-borg's. "Though for the life of me, I don't see the attraction. Not enough mucus." She shuddered. "Once she has broken Star Guy's concentration, his dratted force field will drop, making him vulnerable to a precision strike from my long-range viral agitator."

She resumed her steady procession around the Cara-borg. "We have made a study of Earth's teenage girls. And our robot is programmed to behave just like a typical example. She cannot be bargained with. She cannot be reasoned with. And she absolutely will not stop, ever, until she has tracked down Star Guy and completed her mission." The Overlord circled back in front of the robot. "Cara Marjorie Lee, state your mission objectives."

The Cara-borg stood to attention. "One, locate the superhero known as Star Guy. Two, gain his affection. Three, achieve mass distraction through the use of my onboard osculatory function."

"Her what?" I asked.

The Overlord smiled. "A small modification to your plan. It has been determined by our ratings super-computer that in order to fully distract Star Guy, the robot must engage him in what you humans call . . . *canoodling.*"

"You monsters," I gasped. The sue-dunham were more evil than I could possibly have imagined.

"Yes," said the Overlord. "We are monsters." She loomed over me. "And we're coming to get everyone you love."

I fought rising panic. The sue-dunham had to be stopped, and I was the only one who knew about the invasion. But not for long.

I closed my eyes, and in my head I shouted Zack's

name over and over, trusting that he would pick up my distress call telepathically. I pictured my small voice reaching out through the cosmic darkness. For the sake of billions of human beings, Zack *had* to hear me.

And he did.

"What?" said his grudging voice eventually. "This better be important, Luke. I'm studying for my algebra test."

I took a deep breath and said, "Zack, I'm on board an alien mother ship and they all look like my gym teacher and they're about to launch an invasion using a robot Cara and force us to watch reality shows for the rest of time."

There was a pause. "I told you," said Zack in a low voice. "I warned you what would happen if you clogged up our telepathic connection with more nonsense. That's it, Luke—you're *banned*."

"But, Zack, I'm not—"

Click.

The telepathic link went dead.

He didn't believe me. Typical. Sure, he'd fly to everyone else's rescue at the drop of a cat, but when I needed him? Uh-uh. I was on my own. And now Earth was at the mercy of the sue-dunham.

The Overlord poked the OFF switch on her TV remote, and the floating screen vanished. "Now that you know our plans," she said, "we cannot, of course, permit you to leave the ship and raise the alarm." Two of the sue-dunham separated themselves from the front rank and took me firmly by each arm. "See that our honored guest is made *most comfortable*. Take him to the math block!"

With that, the Overlord leaped onto the pommel horse, puffed out her chest, and cast a bulgy eye across the alien masses. "Prepare for the invasion. Ready the fighter-bombers. Charge the long-range viral agitator. Launch the teenage girl. Today Luke Parker," she crowed, "tomorrow the world."

THE SUM OF ALL FEARS

With the triumphant shriek of alien whistles ringing in my ears, I was escorted from the transporter room/ gymnasium, bound for detention in the math block. The sue-dunham had plugged into my deepest fears: not only did every one of them look like my terrifying gym teacher, but this section of the mother ship was also a replica of my loathed school, right down to the inexplicable smell of cabbage forever wafting through the corridors. Oh, if only the aliens *had* appeared to me as slimy, multiheaded, slavering monsters. *That* I could have coped with. But this? This was the true face of horror.

"Hey," I complained to the guards, "is this any way to treat the Thucwex Gsuphlon?"

Ignoring my protests, they led me deeper into the mother ship. As we passed a row of English classrooms, I was sure I could hear from inside the unmistakable drone of trapped children being forced to recite Shakespeare.

I ventured a peek into one, only to see rows of empty chairs. If the torturous sound was a simulation, its purpose to instill dread, then it was working.

The aliens herded me upstairs to the math block. I tried to engage them in conversation, hoping they might let slip something I could use against them.

"You won't win, whatever the Overlord thinks. Invaders never do," I said, hoping that they hadn't read the limited-series comic crossover *Secret Invasion*, in which the Skrulls nearly succeeded.

The sue-dunham guards ignored me.

"I know you can understand me," I said. "In comics aliens can all speak perfect English because they have some kind of universal translation device implanted in their heads." The guards studied me in curious silence. "One thing puzzles me about your plan. If you can turn yourself into my gym teacher, then I'm guessing you could make yourself look like any human being. So why bother building a robot that looks like Cara when one of you could just turn yourself into a copy of her?"

The guards exchanged looks. I got the feeling they were debating whether to answer my question. Finally, the leader turned to me and in a dull voice droned, "The audience loves an evil robot." It was a fair point. Under different circumstances I could see the appeal.

They didn't utter another word for the remainder of

our march to the math block. We came to a halt outside classroom AA-23.

I'd never been in detention before. Josh Khan got one for not doing his geography homework. He didn't seem to care, swaggering about the next day saying, "If you can't do the time, don't do the crime." Which seemed funny to me, since his detention lasted only fifteen minutes—though he didn't laugh when I pointed that out to him in front of the rest of the class.

The first guard reached into a holster on her belt, drew out another of those TV remotes, and pointed it at the lock. There was the snick of sliding bolts, and then the door swung wide. She bundled me inside, and the door closed automatically behind me. I was a prisoner.

Looking around, I could see that the classroom was identical to the one in my real school except for the view out. Rising above the sports field shone the dizzying band of the Milky Way. I tore myself away—this was no time to be admiring the beauty of the cosmos. The Cara-borg was already heading for Earth to hunt down Star Guy. I needed to figure out a way off this bucket of bolts, and fast.

I scoured the classroom for anything to aid my escape. First I checked the storage cupboard. As I sifted through the items inside, separating any that might prove useful, I was startled by a sound. Someone was humming, faint but clear. I recognized the tune, the chorus to the latest single from the new Billy Dark album. It was coming from behind the teacher's desk at the front of the room. I rounded the desk to find a small grate at the base of the wall; then I dropped to my knees and pressed my ear to listen. I had a strong suspicion about who was at the other end of the duct.

"Cara," I whispered. "Is that you?"

There was a frantic scraping sound and a thud from the other end, and then a familiar voice said, "Who's there?"

"It's me, Luke Parker."

"Kid!" It was Cara, all right. "They got you too, huh?"

It made perfect sense that she'd be imprisoned here. The suc-dunham couldn't have the real Cara Lee getting in the way while their robot copy went about her evil mission.

"What happened to you?" she asked. "I was walking through the park, listening to the new Billy Dark album, and the next thing I knew—"

"There was a green flash and you woke up craving grilled cheese."

"Yeah. And the weirdest thing is, I don't even *like* grilled cheese."

"It's good that you're a prisoner here too," I said.

"It is?" said Cara, puzzled. "Good for who?"

"For all humankind," I said. I had an idea that taking Cara Lee prisoner might prove to be the sue-dunham's undoing. Zack didn't want to hear from *me*, but she was someone he'd *always* take a call from. "Cara, you have to contact Star Guy telepathically."

"I do? Why would he listen to me?"

"He'll listen, trust me. You have to tell him everything. Reach out with your mind. Are you reaching?"

"OK, OK. Here I go." There was a delay that seemed to last forever, and then Cara said excitedly, "It's him! I can hear his voice."

We were saved! Now the aliens would get what was coming to them. My superhero brother would be here in a flash. Oh yeah, the sue-dunham were about to—

"No, wait," said Cara. "It's a recorded message." In a halting voice she repeated it for me. "'Hello, it's Star Guy. I appreciate your call. However, due to the excessive number of mind-to-mind requests I receive, I've had to limit access to my telepathic communication. If you have a PIN, please enter it now. If your request is urgent, or you believe you should be on the approved caller list, then contact the District Council, extension eight six two.' Or it might have been eight six four. It went a bit crackly at the end." Cara sighed. "He's not coming for us, is he?"

"Nope," I said. I didn't have a PIN. I didn't even know

there was an approved caller list. "If we're getting out of here, we're going to have to do it all by ourselves."

"OK, Houdini," she said. "So how exactly do we do that?"

I paced the classroom, deep in thought. Harry Houdini, the famous escapologist, would have freed himself from this place in seconds, with only a smile and a hairpin hidden in his silk underpants. But did I have skills like Houdini? I was about to find out.

"OK, let's review," I said. "All we have to do is escape from detention, evade the hordes of deadly sue-dunham prowling the corridors, make our way back to the transporter in the gym, figure out how to work the controls, and beam ourselves home."

"Right. Simple then," said Cara.

I was glad she agreed. I continued my search for equipment to aid our escape. One of those TV remotes would have been useful. It seemed to be the sue-dunham's version of the Doctor's sonic screwdriver in *Doctor Who*, capable of unlocking doors—and who knew what else. Unfortunately, all I could lay my hands on were a pack of three-ring binders in pastel shades, a handful of thumbtacks, a metal protractor, a triangle, and a dozen plastic rulers. I informed Cara.

"Useful, kid," she said. "If you want to give the aliens a particularly tricky geometry problem."

I twirled the triangle around my finger. "Y'know what, that's not a bad idea."

Five minutes later, everything was in place. Now, for my plan to have any chance of success, I had to attract the attention of the guard outside the door. I could see her outline through the frosted glass.

"Ooooh," I moaned, loud enough for her to hear. "I don't feel well. I think it was the grilled cheese. The room is spinning. I'm going to blow space chunks. *Bleurgh.*"

I kept up my pretend retching until the door swung open and the guard poked her head inside to check on me.

That was her first mistake.

The dozen rulers I'd tacked to the door frame bent back under the action of the opening door and, with a volley of *boings*, pinged against her face. Wincing at the slaps, she stumbled into the room—and the next part of my trap. I had set the binders in a tight pattern across the floor, their stiff metallic rings pried apart like bear traps, ready to clamp onto unwary feet. The guard lurched into the minefield, letting out whistles of pain as dozens of metal pincers nipped at her toes. In an attempt to avoid further injury, she performed a desperate hopping dance that brought her within range of the storage cupboard where I'd secreted myself. From my hiding place

I watched as she teetered on one leg, weakened and off balance. I wouldn't get a better chance.

I sprang from the cupboard. "Hypotenuse *this*," I quipped, bringing the curved metal edge of the pro-tractor down like a pirate cutlass, severing the holster from her belt and spilling the remote control held inside. Catching the falling device, I leaped nimbly over the snapping binders. Once on the other side of the door, I quickly aimed and fired the remote. The door slammed shut, sealing the guard inside.

Seconds later I freed Cara from the classroom next door. She looked down at me. *"Hypotenuse this?"*

I shrugged. "Best I could come up with."

She glanced both ways along the empty corridor. "Come on," she said. "We're not out of this yet."

BAMF!

We headed out of the math block, passing a bulletin board plastered with announcements about guard-duty rosters, the forthcoming invasion, and a bake sale. Next to the board was a long window that overlooked the staff parking lot. A glimpse out revealed the scale of the aliens' invasion preparations. Cara gasped. The parking lot was crowded not with the usual Nissans and Fords, but with sleek atmospheric strike fighters and bombers. If they were anything like the ones in the video game, Earth's military forces would be swept aside.

"How are we going to stop all that?" said Cara.

"We're not," I said. My brother was the only thing that stood between the aliens and Earth's destruction—and only if he stopped being in a huff with me.

We paused at the next junction, pressing our backs to the wall and holding our breath as a patrol marched past. Once they turned the corner, I started to move off. Cara held me back.

"Uh, wasn't that Miss Dunham? And Miss Dunham?"

Cara didn't know about the sue-dunham. It turned out she hadn't seen a soul since being beamed aboard the ship. She only knew that she was in an alien vessel at all because of the glossy magazine slipped under her door, titled *What's On Board!* And the accompanying article, "This Month, Invasion Earth: Ten Things You Never Knew About the Destruction of the Human Race."

As we plotted our way through the maze of corridors, I filled her in on what I'd learned about the aliens—their gym teacher disguise, the reality TV show, the video game trap—and then I got to the part about her robot impostor. That was kind of awkward.

"Wait, why did you make her look like *me?*"

Uh-oh. I felt a slipping sensation, as if this conversation was about to get away from me.

"You could have picked any girl in the world."

"Uh, no, I couldn't," I said quickly. "The game only has people from our town."

"OK, but you could have chosen *any* of them."

The truth, of course, was that I'd had to pick Cara because Zack had a crush on her. But I couldn't exactly tell her that without revealing Star Guy's identity. The possible conversation flashed through my mind:

"I made the robot look like you because Star Guy has a huge crush on you."

"He does? How do you know?"

"Because he's my big brother."

She was studying me with a curious expression, waiting for a response.

There was a whistle from back down the corridor—an alien patrol had spotted us. I'd never been happier in my life to be ambushed. An alarm that sounded like the school bell blared across the deck. Now the whole crew would be looking for us.

"This way!" I shouted, taking Cara's hand and leading her into a stairwell. We bounded downstairs, taking the steps four at a time. Behind us I could hear the beat of alien sneakers as the sue-dunham pursued us as relentlessly as Miss Dunham during cross-country season.

We crashed through the stairwell door, our feet sliding on the polished floor as we came to a halt in the school's entrance foyer. Over the main door hung the school flag, with its Viking ship emblem and Latin motto, *Sit Vis Vobiscum.* But the alien foyer was far bigger than the real one. It had to be in order to house so many trophy cabinets. Instead of the handful of dusty glass cases that lined the corridor outside the main office on Earth, here there were dozens and dozens arranged in tight rows.

"Quick, over here," whispered Cara.

I felt a tug on my collar as she pulled me down behind one of the cabinets. There was the athletic bounce of footsteps as the sue-dunham patrol swept into the entrance foyer from the stairwell. From our hiding place we watched with relief as they jogged past us, into the cafeteria across the corridor.

As they filed inside, my eyes switched focus to the glass cabinet in front of me. Instead of a football trophy or a medal for being the runner-up in volleyball, there sat an unexpected but familiar object.

"It's a TV remote," I said.

"And there's another one in here," said Cara, peering into the next case.

An inspection of more cases revealed remote controls in all of them. Each had a different design. Some appeared to have been fashioned for use with one hand, two, or even three. Others were meant to be held in suckered tentacles or claws, or operated by fingers made of water or pure energy.

Set into the plinth beneath each case was a plaque engraved with alien writing and a pattern of circles and intersecting lines. I ran a finger over the raised design.

"It's a star chart," I said, suddenly realizing what I was looking at. "They're coordinates for different planets." I came to a horrible conclusion. "Each of these remote controls must belong to a race that the aliens have conquered."

We looked slowly around the entrance foyer. There were hundreds of remote control trophies. The sue-dunham had rampaged across galaxies, destroying everything before them, all in the name of a reality TV show.

"And we're next," said Cara quietly.

The full horror of our situation sank in. If the aliens succeeded, then we'd soon be just another TV remote in a glass case.

"What are you doing?!" said Cara, as I lifted off one of the glass tops and removed the remote from inside.

"If it's anything like the sue-dunham's, then maybe we can use it." I pointed it at the main entrance door and tapped the ON button. Nothing. "Batteries must be dead."

I abandoned the remote and headed off with Cara for the gym. I was sure that at any moment a sue-dunham patrol would pounce on us, but we reached the end of the corridor unscathed. We peeked around the corner.

The entrance to the gym lay before us. Unfortunately, so did a solid line of guards. My heart sank. There was no way we were getting past them.

Cara turned to me. "Look, kid, one of us has to get off this ship and warn Star Guy," she said. "But not both of us. I'll create a diversion while you get to the beaming thingy and head back to Earth."

"But—"

Cara suddenly looked furious. "The aliens took my phone," she said. "And *no one* takes my phone." She said it the way the Thing says, "It's clobbering time." Part of me felt scared for the alien invaders.

"Kid, if I don't make it, tell Matthias . . . I really, really liked him."

I winced. *Do I have to?* Under the circumstances I felt I ought to agree. I nodded.

She took a deep breath and stepped into the corridor. Waving her arms and yelling at the top of her lungs, she charged at the guards. Taken by surprise, they turned and ran, whistling their dismay as the fearless Cara chased them off down the corridor. Soon they would realize they were being hounded not by the Howling Commandos, but by an unarmed teenage girl looking for her cell phone. Dangerous as that was, it wouldn't stop them for long. I had to go. Now.

A low hum of power filled the near-empty gym. One side of the pommel horse had been removed, exposing a bank of intricate alien machinery. It had to be the controls for the matter transporter. A lone sue-dunham performed what I guessed to be a series of diagnostic tests on the equipment. Focused on her work, she failed to spot me lurking at the door. She adjusted several dials, tapped a sequence of keys, and studied a readout on a display. She noted something on a handheld device before disappearing through another door into the sports equipment storage room. Now was my chance.

I stood before the baffling control panel. To my dismay it looked nothing like the one in the transporter room on the starship *Enterprise*. I felt like a monkey put in charge of the Large Hadron Collider. This was bad. I could take a guess and start hitting random controls, but in comics, teleportation was notoriously dangerous. I'd be meddling with the fabric of space-time; one wrong input and I could end up beaming myself into the side of a mountain, or a dimension populated by bloodsucking giraffes. Or worse.

Fishing out the TV remote I'd snatched from the guard, I studied the symbols on its buttons. Every remote control in our house had a button that brought up a help menu. I pushed the likeliest candidate.

A 3-D holographic image of a book appeared above the pommel horse, accompanied by a jumble of noises that I quickly realized were lots of different languages. The system seemed to be searching through them. Finally, it stopped and a woman's voice said in perfect

English, "Congratulations on choosing the UniBeamer 500, the latest in interpersonal matter transportation. With the proper care and maintenance, the UniBeamer 500 will provide you with years of trouble-free teleporting pleasure. This beamer is sold with a five-year guarantee—valid only if repairs are made at an authorized spaceport using genuine parts. Guarantee not valid in the Horsehead Nebula."

The holographic manual opened to the contents page. I scanned the list for the quick-start section.

As I searched for the instructions I racked my brains. What did I know about teleportation? I knew that when Nightcrawler did it in comics, it made a sound like *bamf* and left behind a whiff of brimstone. Most teleportation devices that I'd read about needed a target. Something to lock on to. So how had they targeted me? When the sue-dunham had beamed me up, I'd been in Crystal Comics playing *Puny Earthlings!*

The game disc.

Of course. The spiderweb of circuitry beneath the surface wasn't some kind of graphic design; it was *actual* circuitry. The disc had to be part of the teleporter. That way the aliens could beam up whoever was playing the game.

There had to be something in the manual about targeting. I combed through it until I found the right section. I had to read it twice—it was even more complicated than the instructions for my LEGO Star Wars AT-AT Walker. Crossing my fingers, I tapped a control on the main pommel horse panel. A map appeared before me like a genie from a lamp. I recognized my town immediately.

A second later the map was overlaid with hundreds of disc-shaped symbols that speckled the area like measles, one for every household where the sue-dunham had planted a copy of their fiendish video game.

If I understood the manual correctly, I could teleport anywhere on the map with a disc symbol just by touching it.

I hesitated. The sue-dunham would be able to track me using the teleporter's equivalent of the last number dialed. They'd be sure to follow me to Earth. Once there I'd need help to keep them off my back while I tracked down Zack and convinced him of the imminent invasion. This was exactly the kind of mission S.C.A.R.F. was designed to handle. But S.C.A.R.F. was no more than a rejected logo in a portfolio case.

I zoomed in on the map. I needed someone with experience. Someone familiar with evil, world-dominating plans. There was only one man for the job.

I prodded the glowing disc symbol on Main Street.

A whine rose from the pommel horse as the teleporter charged up, and then a shaft of green light shone down from the roof, bathing the top panel of the horse. It was the transporter beam—my bus home.

From the other end of the gym came a screech of outrage. The transporter's start-up sequence had alerted the sue-dunham operator. She sprinted from the equipment storeroom, brandishing a lacrosse net, whistle clenched between her teeth. I had seconds to get to the beam.

I swung a leg up onto the pommel horse, but only succeeded in banging my knee against the side. It was too high. If I was going to get off this ship and save Earth, then I had to do something I'd never accomplished: a perfect vault. I took a few steps back, closed my eyes, drew a deep breath, and remembered Miss Dunham's words from gym class: "*Knees high and spring.*"

I felt my feet pound against the floor, my hands set firmly against the suede top, and then I lifted off like the *Millennium Falcon* blasting out of Mos Eisley Spaceport. The whine reached a terrible crescendo, like the school orchestra rehearsing. There was a bright green flash.

And I was no longer in the room.

I hurtled through darkness at incomprehensible speeds, but at the same time I felt as if I was moving through water. Stars blurred, galaxies swirled, space folded. Who knew what dimensions I was traveling through or where I was headed? In the murk of space-time I glimpsed a shape.

Quickly it became a figure. It was me, but not me. He stood with hands on hips, chin thrust outward, a cape fluttering from his back, a set of stars glowing on his chest. I didn't understand. Who? How? Where?

And then I had a sudden and overwhelming need to eat a grilled cheese sandwich.

SUPERVILLAIN TEAM-UP

"I'm not paying you to sit here and play *Space Invaders* all day," said a faraway voice.

Blearily, I opened my eyes to see Christopher Talbot standing over me.

"Just to be clear," he went on, "I'm *not* paying you, but if I were, then it wouldn't be to play computer games. Well, what have you to say for yourself?"

"I'm not in an evil giraffe dimension," I mumbled.

He folded his arms. "OK, one out of ten for sense, but I'll give you the full ten for weirdness."

I was still woozy from the teleportation, but I could see that I'd made it back to Crystal Comics. There wasn't much time—the aliens would be right behind me. I had to explain everything to Christopher Talbot and warn Zack without delay.

Too late. A green glow enveloped the Xbox, and

a swirl of atoms appeared in the beam.

They were coming.

"You know anything about this?" said Christopher Talbot, poking an investigative finger at the beam.

"Don't!" I cried, reaching for my alien remote. It wasn't there. In the chaos of the escape I must have left it behind. "We have to get out of here. Now."

Before I could move, the atoms took the shape of a tracksuited sue-dunham. She stepped from the beam onto the floor of the comic book store. Immediately, she was followed by another. Behind them I could see a third forming. Instead of the usual light-blue tracksuit, each wore a matte black version, and their silver whistles were smudged with camouflage paint to reduce reflections. Just as I'd expected: the Overlord had sent a squad of Special Forces gym teachers to hunt me down.

Christopher Talbot threw me a questioning look.

"I was on an alien spaceship, and I may, accidentally, have brought about the end of the world. I didn't mean to," I added hurriedly.

He shrugged. "Happens to the best of us."

The sue-dunham commandos raised their remote controls.

Christopher Talbot gave a reluctant sigh. "I was saving this. But desperate times . . ."

He thrust out a hand and flared his fingers.

There was a howl, like a hurricane and a tornado having a fight, and the aliens sailed toward the back wall of the store. With a succession of thuds they slid to the floor, stunned but alive. One of them vanished in a cloud of glowing particles. I think she must have been damaged, and some automatic recovery system had beamed her back to the mother ship. That left two.

I knew instantly what had happened. "You lied to me," I stuttered, turning an accusing stare on Christopher Talbot. "The asteroid. It *did* give you superpowers."

He looked at me like I was an idiot. "Of course it did. Some kind of energy field. My theory is that Nemesis had a nickel-iron core—y'know, the stuff they used to make rechargeable batteries from. And somehow the power was transferred to me." He studied his hands. "I'm thinking of calling myself the Energizer."

It was a terrible name, but at that moment I didn't care. The sue-dunham were already getting to their feet. "Can you do it again?" I asked.

"Takes about an hour to recharge," he said, running for the door. Fleetingly, I registered that he wasn't using his cane anymore. He paused in the doorway. "Well, don't just stand there. Move it! I can't have those aliens blasting you to atoms. Not before *I've* had my chance to blast you."

"Are you saying what I think you're saying?"

"Yes," he said grimly. "Until they're defeated, looks like we're on the same team."

I scrambled after him, and we raced out onto Main Street. Christopher Talbot was a whirl of pumping arms and legs. I struggled to keep up. He hurdled a line of kindergartners. "But just to be clear, Luke, the first chance I get, I'm going to double-cross you and take my revenge on you and your annoying brother."

At least I knew where I stood. He dashed across the road to the angry honks of passing cars.

"But you always said you wanted to be a super*hero*," I said, catching up with him once again.

"That dream is over," he said, clipping the elbow of a charity collector and knocking the money can out of his hand. "And I have you to thank for putting me on my true evil path."

Me?

"As you so ably pointed out during our epic confrontation in my former volcano lair, I am a much better villain than a hero."

I felt a sudden and terrible weight on my shoulders. I was responsible for giving the aliens the key to taking over Earth, and I had turned Christopher Talbot to the dark side. And it wasn't even lunchtime.

"In here," he cried.

We ducked into Marshalls, and he made directly for

a rack of clothes in the clearance section.

"So, what exactly are we dealing with?" he asked, flicking through an assortment of jackets and cardigans.

"A squad of alien shock troops, sent in advance of the main invasion by an evil overlord on a cloaked mother ship disguised as an ordinary junior high school in geosynchronous orbit above the highway at the corner of Brewery Road. And it's all part of an intergalactic reality TV show."

"OK."

I'd been counting on him catching on quickly, but I was still surprised at how well he took the news. "So you believe me?"

"I've just been assaulted by cloned gym teachers who materialized out of an Xbox. Let's say I'm keeping an open mind." He thrust a cardigan at me. "Here, put this on."

"For a disguise?"

"No, because the blue brings out your eyes."

I pulled on the cardigan as he slipped into a tweed jacket. Finally, he handed me a stripy wool hat with a pom-pom on top. Normally, I wouldn't wear anything with a pom-pom, but these weren't normal circumstances. I had a horrible thought. If he was willing to team up with *me*, then . . . "You're not going to do some sort of supervillain deal with the aliens, are you?"

"Well, I wasn't," he said. "But now that you mention it—"

"No! I didn't mean—"

"Yes," he mused. "Once they've taken over the world with my help, they're sure to reward me. Perhaps I'll ask for Bavaria. I've always had a weakness for *zwetschgenkuchen*. It's a short-crust pie covered with pitted *zwetschge*." He gave me a withering look. "Oh, come on, Luke, what do you take me for? Team up with alien invaders—when has that *ever* worked out for the villain?"

He was right. I'd never read a single comic in which alien invaders stuck to their promises.

We joined a line to pay for the new clothes. "And anyway, I'm not the one who gave the Martians the nuclear codes, or whatever it was you did up there." He paused. "What exactly *did* you do up there?"

I fiddled guiltily with my pom-pom. Swiftly, I explained the situation with the Cara-borg sent to distract Star Guy. Just as I finished, there was the screech of a whistle from behind the new season's monochrome checkered jackets. One of the sue-dunham commandos had found us.

"Let's get out of here!" I yelled, but Christopher Talbot had already gone. We hadn't been a team for long, but I'd already noticed that at the first sniff of danger, he didn't exactly hang around.

"We need to find your brother before that robot girl gets her lips on him," he said as we burst through the door back onto Main Street.

"I know where he'll be," I said. I glanced back to see a security guard tackle the sue-dunham in a tassel-print wrap dress that she hadn't paid for. That would buy us some time.

It didn't take long to reach our destination. The slab-sided battleship that was the Central Library reared up before us.

We dashed inside to begin our search for Zack. "He's probably in the section with all the math books," I said. "Let's start there."

"Lead on, Macduff," said Christopher Talbot with a grin.

I thought that in all the excitement he must have forgotten my name, but I didn't correct him. He loped up the staircase, three stairs at a time, fizzing with energy and happier than I'd seen him since he'd stepped into his Mark Fourteen Super Suit, ready to do battle with Nemesis. A dose of danger and the prospect of revenge had made him perkier than a pig with a jetpack. I was glad, at least for now. I needed all the help I could get if I was going to stop the aliens.

Zack wasn't among the math books. As we continued to the next floor, the sheer scale of our challenge struck me. Zack had been obsessed with Cara since the day she'd moved onto our street. The robot was a flawless copy of my brother's dream girl, programmed to love him. As far as he knew, she *was* Cara. This wasn't Mission: Impossible; it was harder than that.

If I was going to save the world, I had to stop Zack from kissing Cara.

SHH!

We reached the next floor and swung through the doors into the silent room beyond. A librarian in a purple dress and big boots rolled a squeaky cart loaded with books across the floor. I spotted Zack immediately—he was the only other person in the place. He sat at a table under a window, his back toward me. I was about to call out to him, but before I could open my mouth, a long shadow fell across the library floor. There was a whisper of track-suited legs as one of the sue-dunham Special Forces burst through the door with an earsplitting shriek from her whistle.

"Shh," hushed the librarian.

The sue-dunham aimed her remote control at us and fired.

I clutched my chest, fingers prodding for the expected blast hole, but I was still in one piece. She must have missed. Christopher Talbot raised his arms in surrender. For someone with superpowers, he wasn't exactly over-flowing with bravery.

While she held him in her cold gym teacher's gaze, I seized my chance. Bolting across the room, I had one thought: to warn Zack. Approaching his table by the window, I saw that he was plugged into his phone, and I remembered that he liked to listen to podcasts about famous mathematicians while he studied. I tugged out his earbuds and he spun around in surprise.

"Luke," he said. "What are you doing here?"

Out of the corner of my eye, I watched a beanbag in the shape of a dragon sail across the library, as the sue-dunham commando chased Christopher Talbot through the children's section. And in turn they were both pursued by the librarian.

"There's an alien fleet poised to invade Earth, and you're being hunted by a robot that looks like Cara" was what I tried to tell Zack, but what came out was . . .

Silence.

I tried to speak again, but the only sound was the flapping of my lips.

With horror I realized what must have happened. The sue-dunham hadn't missed her target at all. Her remote control had been set to MUTE.

I was about to contact Zack telepathically when I

remembered he'd blocked me. I raged in silence.

With a huff of impatience Zack turned his back on me and returned to his studying, just as Christopher Talbot wheeled by, riding atop the librarian's cart, hurling books off the back of it at the pursuing commando.

Zack didn't see a thing. I tugged urgently at his sleeve.

"Luke, what is *wrong* with you?"

With no other way to communicate, I'd have to write down what was going on. I searched his desk in vain—there was never a uni-ball Gelstick when you needed one. I thought fast. There was one man who could help me—and I knew exactly where to find him. Grabbing hold of Zack's sleeve, I hauled him deeper into the leather-bound quiet of the library.

"Hey, get off!" he yelled, but I wouldn't let go. As we sped past lines of neatly stacked books, I scanned the spines for their authors. Vance . . . Verne . . . Vonnegut . . . *Almost there.* The next row. *Got it!* The author's name shone from the book like a lighthouse in a storm—on Mars.

H. G. Wells.

I plucked the slim volume from its shelf and thrust it into my brother's hands. He read the title with a puzzled frown.

"*The War of the Worlds?*"

In the absence of a book titled *We're Being Invaded by*

Aliens and Your Next-Door Neighbor Is an Evil Robot, this would have to do.

"You want me to read it?" he asked. I nodded furiously. "I don't have time for this. I have my first exam in"—he checked his watch—"less than twenty-three months." I flipped the book open and jammed it into his face. When I was little my dad had read *War of the Worlds* to me as a bedtime story. Since it had left me with nightmares about heat rays and choking red weed, I remembered every word. I stabbed a finger halfway down the first page.

"OK, OK, if it means so much to you." He cleared his throat and began. *"Yet, across the gulf of space . . . intellects vast and cool and unsympathetic, regarded this earth with envious eyes, and slowly and surely drew their plans against us."* He looked up. "So what?"

Gah! How difficult was it to deduce a full-blown alien invasion from a line out of a groundbreaking nineteenth-century science-fiction novel? And he was supposed to be the smart one.

"Hey, isn't that Miss Dunham?" said Zack.

The alien look-alike stood at the end of the aisle. Luckily, she hadn't yet spotted us.

"She wants me on track, y'know." Zack preened. "I wasn't going to bother, but then I found out that Cara's on the girls' team." He made a strange gurgling sound in his throat, and before I could stop him he had raised a hand and was waving to attract her attention. "Hey, Miss Dun—*oof!*"

I bundled him to the floor and clamped a hand over his mouth. He continued to complain in a muffled voice. I ventured a glance over my shoulder. The sue-dunham's terrible blank eyes met mine. I found myself staring straight down the business end of her remote control. No way she would miss. What would it be this time? Heat ray? Shrink ray? I braced myself.

Suddenly, there was a mighty shushing noise like a great gust in a forest, and the commando was swatted aside by a purple blur. It was the librarian. She hurled herself at the alien, and the two of them crashed into the Travel and Tourism section. The bookcase wobbled and, creaking under the weight of all those atlases, fell on top of the struggling duo. When the dust settled, the librarian arose triumphant. All that was visible of the alien were her sneakered feet poking out, like the Wicked Witch of the East squished beneath Dorothy's house. There was a faint crackle, and then the alien's automatic recovery system activated and she vanished in a cloud of glimmering particles—the same thing that had happened to her compatriot in Crystal Comics. With a thud the bookshelf fell the last few inches to the floor. Two down. That left one more commando out there. Somewhere.

Pinned beneath me, Zack hadn't seen a thing. "I've had enough of this," he said sharply. I felt myself rise into the air. He was using his superpowers on me! Once clear, he leaped up, brushed himself off, and struck off down the aisle, leaving me hovering at eye level with the dusty top of the bookcase, shouting mute warnings after him. From my position I could see all the way to the door, where Lara now entered. Perhaps I'd have better luck explaining the emergency to her.

I felt the telekinetic strings vanish, and thumped to the ground with a silent *ouch*. Picking myself up, I hobbled out from between the stacks to find Zack at his reading table. Lara stood next to him, her head half-buried in a paper bag.

"They didn't have tuna, so I got you chicken salad." She dug into the bag. "Hey, Luke," she said, noticing me. "What are you doing here?"

"Forget about him," said Zack, jumping up and clutching his head. He squeezed his eyes shut as he concentrated. "My Star Screen is picking up a disturbance. I'm getting a strong visual. The mall. People running and screaming. Lots of frightened faces." His eyes flicked open. "Cara."

"My sister's in danger?" Lara dropped the sandwich bag and snatched up the gym bag containing her costume. "What are we waiting for?"

I shook my head. "It's not her," I shouted in vain. "It's a trap." I stepped in front of Zack, blocking his path.

"Luke, what are you doing? Cara needs me." He blushed. "I mean, she needs Star Guy."

He pushed me aside and they dashed for the door. I set off after them, knowing I could never keep up with the superpowered duo. I was halfway to the exit when I heard Christopher Talbot's voice boom across the library, and abruptly fall silent.

"Give that device to me; its technology is way beyond your meager understand—"

Click.

I rounded Geography, bolted past Warfare, and skidded to a stop in front of Body and Mind. There stood Christopher Talbot and the purple librarian, wrestling each other for the alien's remote control. So far, it was a one-sided contest. The librarian must have seized it when she took care of the alien commando. I was impressed. I made a mental note never again to be late returning a book.

Click.

"I warn you, madam," said Christopher Talbot. "If you do not relinquish that alien artifact, I shall have no option but to—"

Click.

As amusing as it was to watch Christopher Talbot

turn mauve with anger, there wasn't time to let it continue. I snatched the device from her eager fingers and ran for the door. Christopher Talbot caught up with me in a few bounds. Two clicks later, we had our voices back. As we pounded downstairs, I filled him in on what happened with Zack.

"They think they're rushing off to perform a heroic rescue," I explained as we raced out of the library and back onto the street. "But they're about to walk right into the middle of an alien cyborg kissing ambush."

We sped along Main Street, threading our way through shoals of office workers, dodging knuckle-dragging teenagers with their heads bent over their phones, all the way to the mall. But before we'd even made it past Walgreens, the third alien commando stepped out of the crowd.

THE PERFECT KISSING MACHINE

The sue-dunham Special Forces gym teacher stood with her feet shoulder-width apart, knees slightly bent, arms hanging relaxed at her sides—a lot like the stance Miss Dunham had demonstrated when teaching us how to throw a basketball. Her eyes locked onto us like a missile-guidance system. Pedestrians flowed around her, unaware of the alien terror in their midst.

"Has your battery recharged?" I asked Christopher Talbot.

"Not yet," he said.

"It's not the best superpower ever, is it?"

"No," he agreed glumly.

And then something remarkable happened. Christopher Talbot's expression hardened. He straightened to his full height, dropped his hands to his hips, and waggled his fingers. He was preparing for either a free throw or a showdown.

"Luke, you have to go," he said quietly.

"But what about you?"

He surveyed the sue-dunham commando coldly. "I've got this."

I could hardly believe it—he was choosing to be a hero instead of a villain. "But without your power, how will you—"

"Never mind that." He paused. "If I don't make it, Luke, it's up to you and your little friends."

"We're called S.C.A.R.F.," I said.

He threw me a doubtful look. "S.C.A.R.F.? *Really?*"

"I'd like to see you come up with a better name," I muttered.

"What are you waiting for?" He glowered. "Get out of here before I change my mind."

I took off without another word. Merging with the crowd, I glanced back to see them square up to one another like a couple of Wild West gunslingers. As I hurried past Kay Jewelers, all the clocks in the window chimed noon. I hoped Christopher Talbot knew what he was doing.

The mall was just off Main Street. A stray chunk of the Nemesis asteroid had demolished part of it, but reconstruction was well under way, and it wasn't all bad, since they were opening an Apple store. I arrived outside the main entrance to find it jammed with hordes of screaming people. They weren't lining up for the latest iPhone.

Panicking shoppers stampeded out onto the street, bursting the doors off their hinges in their desperation to escape whatever was inside.

I pushed against the tide, squeezing past into the big, bright central atrium, now empty of people. Easy listening jazz played through the mall's public address system, punctuated by announcements for coming events and special offers. Daylight streamed through the soaring glass roof. It reflected off the splintered glass of broken store windows, and highlighted bags full of new purchases abandoned across the white tiled floor.

It also dazzled off the cube-shaped head of a giant robot in the food court.

The robot stood thirty feet tall, with legs made for stomping, pile-driver arms, and clawed hands for crushing. What I guessed to be its electrohydraulic drive system made whirring and clunking noises as the robot lumbered across the mall floor. With its highly polished casing and retro styling, the robot had clearly been designed by the sue-dunham to look good on TV.

One great claw-hand swatted at the swooping Star Guy, who flew around its head like an annoying gnat.

Its other hand clutched the screaming figure of the Cara-borg.

"Help me, Star Guy!" she yelled, hammering her fists against the metal monstrosity. Her screams were as fake as her synthetic skin. The Overlord had fashioned the fake Cara as surely as she had bolted together the giant robot aboard the mother ship.

"I'll save you, Cara!" Zack called out, before hurriedly corrected himself. "I mean, I'll save you . . . member of the public I have only met briefly once before." He dived at the robot, narrowly dodging the colossal claw as it raked the air.

I wasn't the only one watching the epic confrontation. Lara stood outside Mrs. Fields Cookies, dressed in her Dark Flutter costume.

"Uh, Dark Flutter, shouldn't you be helping Star Guy?"

"My animal power isn't much use in here," she said with a wistful look. "The mall only allows in guide dogs, and I don't think it would be appropriate, firing Labradors at a giant robot."

I agreed that it would not.

Star Guy used his force field to deflect a mighty punch. The robotic fist bounced off wildly, smashing through the window of YO! Sushi. When the robot yanked it back out of the restaurant, there was a selection of sushi and hand rolls along the length of its arm.

"I don't know if you've noticed," said Lara, "but there's a strength and grace to Zack these days. I think he's really coming into his powers."

"That's nice," I grunted. I couldn't bear hearing about Zack's growth as a superhero. As painful as it was for me to admit, it was clear that the robot didn't stand a chance against my brother. The battle would soon be over, and the Cara-borg would deliver its kissy-faced payload. And there was nothing I could do about it.

A discarded shopping bag floated past in the food court fountain.

Or was there?

"Where are you going?" said Lara as I dashed off. "You'll miss the end."

The bag was from the party store just around the corner. I made my way past the princesses and the Star Wars figures, to the superhero section. It didn't take long to find what I needed. Racks of Star Guy costumes had been placed out prominently in time for Halloween. I grabbed one and hurriedly pulled it on; then I checked that everything looked just right in an Evil Queen Magic Mirror. I really looked good as a superhero. "Now who's the coolest of them all?" I said.

"Star Guy," replied the mirror annoyingly.

When I returned to the food court, the fight was in its final throes. Zack and the robot had moved to the upper floor and were going at it toe-to-giant-metal-toe outside Peet's Coffee and Tea.

"Uh, Luke?" said Lara, looking me up and down. "Never mind." She gestured to Zack. "Between you and me, he could've finished this ages ago. He's just showing off. You know what he's like around my sister."

"That's not your sister," I said. "It's a Cara-borg."

"What are you talking about? Of course it's my sister."

There was no time to explain. I had to stop Zack from defeating the giant robot and winning that kiss.

With a toss of his head, Zack adjusted his cape and extended both arms. He was about to bring down the robot using his telekinetic superpower.

"Here it comes," said Lara breathlessly. "The *cow de grass*."

Zack glanced at the Peet's storefront and then back at the robot. "*Hasta la barista,* baby," he quipped.

Even his quips were better than mine!

Swiftly pulling out the alien remote control, I pointed it at myself and prodded the volume switch to its maximum setting.

"*HEY!*" My voice blasted through the mall like a sonic boom.

Store windows that had so far escaped destruction shattered, and the public address system exploded with a shriek of static. The force sent Zack spinning through the air.

But I was too slow. He had already unleashed his superpower. The robot's massive head tumbled off its shoulders and fell, splashing into the food court fountain far below. A shower of sparks accompanied the sharp smell of burning circuitry. Its red electronic eye flickered weakly.

On the upper floor of the mall, the headless torso sank to its knees, releasing its grip on the Cara-borg. Zack took an eager step toward her, failing to notice that the robot was down but not out. The body twitched and one gleaming claw-hand scythed through the air, walloping Zack with the force of a runaway locomotive. With a cry he pitched over the railing and fell. Moments before smashing against the hard tiles, he leveled out and brought himself in for a bouncy landing. He rolled and skidded, finally coming to a stop in a dazed heap at my feet.

In the fountain the robot's red eye flickered one last time and fell dim. That still left the Cara-borg. Leaping over my sprawling brother, I sprinted up the escalator.

The Cara-borg was waiting at the top. "Star Guy? You seem . . . different."

I caught my breath. "I look taller when I'm flying."

The Cara-borg accepted my explanation with a nod. "Oh, Star Guy, if you hadn't rescued me from the clutches

of that *thing*, I don't know what would've become of me."
She sidled closer. "You're so amazing. And powerful.
And *handsome*. If only there was some way I could thank
you." She formed her lips into a pout, closed her eyes,
and lowered her face to mine. It was like the Death Star
approaching Alderaan.

There was nothing I could do about it—I was going to
get kissed. But better me than my brother. I braced myself.

"Tell me this isn't happening," said Zack.

He stood at the top of the escalator with Lara. The
Cara-borg's eyes popped open. She turned her surprised
gaze from me to him. With the real superhero for com-
parison, she saw through my disguise immediately.

"Don't let her kiss you!" I blurted.

Zack stared daggers at me, then turned to the Cara-
borg. "Sorry about him."

"Don't ignore me! You have to listen."

"Uh, no, I don't, actually."

"Are you two related?" asked the Cara-borg suspiciously. "Because you argue just like me and my sis."

"We don't argue that much," objected Lara, and then
realized she'd given the game away. "And by *we*, I mean
me and my . . . three older brothers . . . and my dog . . .
um . . . Patricia."

Lara needn't have worried. The Cara-borg only had
evil cyborg eyes for me and Star Guy.

"Who? Him? My brother?" said Zack. "Nooo. Some fanboy. Probably. Now, how about we get you home. You've had quite a day, Miss . . . ?"

"Call me Cara," said the Cara-borg. "Would you fly me home?"

"I . . . don't usually . . . I mean . . . *sure*." Awkwardly, he extended an arm. "Do you mind if I . . . ? What I mean is . . . purely for safety reasons, I need to . . ."

The Cara-borg took his arm and placed it firmly around her waist. "Like this, Star Guy?"

Below his mask Zack's cheeks flushed. "Yes," he said, in a strangled voice. "Just like that."

Holding the Cara-borg, Star Guy sprang into the air. They flew straight up through the broken atrium roof.

"No! Wait!" I called out, but if he heard, then my brother was ignoring me.

"Luke!" called a voice from below. I peered over the railing, and to my surprise saw Christopher Talbot running up the escalator. Somehow he'd made it past the alien commando.

"What's *he* doing here?" said Lara.

"It's a long story," I said. "And we don't have time to go into it."

Christopher Talbot surveyed the wreckage. "Don't tell me I missed a giant robot battle?"

"Come on," I shouted, scrambling over the debris

toward a door marked ROOF ACCESS ONLY. Maybe there was still time.

"I know you," said Christopher Talbot, studying Lara. "You're the little reporter girl." He snapped his fingers as he tried to recall her name. "Lisa . . . Lois . . . *Laura*."

"Lara," said Lara tightly. "And there goes my secret identity."

"So *you're* Dark Flutter. How intriguing," he said, turning to me. "All these children with superpowers, but not you, Luke. Bet that's annoying."

I gritted my teeth and ignored his teasing. My legs burned as I climbed the stairs. I swore to myself that before the next threat to Earth came around, I'd get in shape.

The door to the roof lay before us. I pushed on the metal bar and shouldered my way outside.

The wind whipped across the flat roof. Below us lay the sprawling town center. With relief I saw my brother over on the other side of the building. Zack and the Cara-borg were cozied up next to a parapet. We raced across the roof. There were only seconds left to neutralize the Cara-borg.

I turned to Christopher Talbot. "Battery power?"

"Still charging," he said with a sigh.

Zack caught sight of the approaching Christopher Talbot, and his lip curled into a sneer. "You!" he snarled, staring into the face of his old enemy.

"Hello, Star Guy. Nice cape." Christopher Talbot picked up an end and rubbed it between two fingers. "Is there some cashmere in this?"

Zack snatched it out of his hand and glowered at both of us. "What's he doing here?"

"I'll explain later," I said. "Right now we need to talk."

"So talk," said Zack.

I glanced at the Cara-borg. She studied me with her emotionless processor eyes. "Over here," I said. "Out of the wind." Taking my brother by the elbow, I steered him out of sensor range of the robot. Christopher Talbot and Lara huddled around us.

"Cara's not who you think she is," I whispered. "She's a robot impostor. And whatever you do, don't let her kiss you or you'll be distracted and the Alien Overlord will fire her long-range viral agitator and it'll be the end of the world."

"Kiss me?" said Zack in a tingly voice.

"Really?" said Christopher Talbot. "Robot impostor? Alien Overlord? End of the world? *No?*"

"You have to believe us," I pleaded.

"Us?" replied Zack.

"Don't look at me," said Lara, taking a step away from me.

"I know it seems . . . unlikely," I said, including Christopher Talbot with a gesture, "but we've teamed up to fight the aliens."

"What aliens?" Zack looked at me like I was nuts. I'd been seeing this expression a lot lately. "I don't see any green, bug-eyed monsters."

"They don't look like green, bug-eyed monsters," I said.

"Then what do they look like?"

I paused and then mumbled, "Miss Dunham."

I decided it would be wise to hold back the bit about the whole invasion being a reality TV show.

"I don't know what's going on here, and right now I don't care," he said, with an air of finality.

"Star Guy, can we go?" The Cara-borg hugged her arms to her body. "I'm getting cold."

Zack marched over and placed an arm around her. Finally, he turned to me and said, "And for the last time, stop bothering me at work."

There was a whoosh of splitting air as the two of them shot into the sky. I watched helplessly as the Cara-borg placed her free hand around the back of Zack's head and pulled his masked face toward her. Her cold cyborg lips homed in on his.

I heard Lara's puzzled voice at my side. "But she's got a boyfriend."

The Cara-borg kissed him.

They bobbed in the breeze for a moment. Far below, the world carried on as usual. Shoppers trawled for bargains. Buses grumbled along Main Street.

A heartbeat later, I flinched as a bright green bolt of light split the sky. Silently, it arrowed down from its orbital weapons platform to strike Star Guy squarely between the shoulder blades. The flash seared my retinas, leaving a shadow across my vision. When it lifted I saw a shape falling out of the sky.

It was my brother plummeting to earth.

ACHOO!

"Mom," called Zack, his voice thin and reedy, "can I have another pillow?"

I stood on the landing outside his bedroom, listening to him cough and sniffle.

Zack wasn't dead. We'd found him lying next to some Dumpsters in an alley behind the mall. The fall hadn't broken any bones, and other than a twisted ankle, he seemed at first to be unharmed, if a little shaken. But the aliens' long-range viral agitator turned out to be a fiendishly clever device, with a far more twisted purpose than any of us could have dreamed. Not a death ray, or a heat ray, or even a shrink ray.

"Achoo!" There was a wet thud as a wad of stringy mucus blew out the back of a man-size tissue.

It was a snot ray.

By the time we brought him home yesterday afternoon, the true nature of the alien weapon had revealed itself in all its catarrh-drenched wickedness. The beam that brought down Zack was a flu shot. And it had given him a bout powerful enough to lay him up in bed for days. I could hear the Overlord's mocking laughter—at Earth's greatest defender, reduced to watching the invasion of the planet on daytime TV.

As for what had happened to the threatened invasion, I was mystified. Why hadn't it started yet? Star Guy was down. His superpowers hadn't gone, exactly, but they were submerged in a soup of phlegm. The greatest obstacle to the sue-dunham's plans was currently tucked in bed with one nostril clamped onto a decongestant spray. Right about now the sky should have been filled with alien attack ships, the streets ringing with the screams of fleeing humans. If I were the Overlord, I wouldn't hang around—there'd be plenty of time to gloat afterward. It didn't make sense. What were the aliens waiting for?

"Mommm!" Zack called again.

"Coming, sweetheart!" She hurried past me, clutching a fresh pillow and muttering, "I didn't think anyone could be worse than your dad."

It was true. Dad was an awful patient, but a superhero with a cold is the worst. As soon as Zack's butt hit the mattress, his demands had started. Theraflu, but not too lemony. And soup: chicken soup, not tomato soup, but not the chicken soup with bits in it, and not the one from the corner store, the one from the deli. Another blanket. But not the blue one.

Mom paused outside his door. "It's a touch of the flu." She raised her eyebrows. "You'd think it was the end of the world."

Little did she know.

Fixing a smile on her face, she went into his room. I followed behind at a cautious distance. The curtains were drawn, and the air was thick with a scent like cooked socks. Zack lay shivering in bed, wrapped in his comforter like an Egyptian mummy. I could just imagine the kind of mummy he'd have been: "I want a pyramid, but not too pyramid-y." On his bedside table lay a pile of textbooks and a bowl of fruit.

"Here you are, darling," said Mom, gently cradling his head and slipping the pillow underneath. "Looks like you'll be missing the big event."

For a moment I thought she meant the invasion.

"Heck of a way to get out of a wedding," she said, plumping up the pillow.

Of course. In all the business with the sue-dunham I'd forgotten about my cousin Jenny's wedding. It was tomorrow, and my brother had evaded it easier than an F-35 spoofing a ground-to-air missile attack. Zack shot me a sly grin. This was *so* unfair.

"Mrs. Wilson will be here to look after you," said

Mom. "And if you need us, my phone will be on."

He laid his head against the fresh pillow, first one way, then the other, all the while making little grumbling noises.

"Something wrong, sweetheart?" asked Mom.

"It's a bit too . . ." He paused. "Feathery."

Instead of whacking him about the head with the pillow, which is what any reasonable person would have done at this point, Mom just smiled. She yanked it out from under him, saying, "Fine, *darling*. I'll fetch you another one."

"Thanks, Mom," he wheezed after her, as she walked quickly from the room. "You're the best."

The door slammed shut, rattling his "Famous Mathematicians" poster set on the wall. Sir Isaac Newton came off his hook and landed in the fruit bowl. I wondered if it was the first time that Newton had fallen on an apple.

"What do you want?" moaned Zack, turning his bloodshot eyes to me. "I'm sick. I can't be bothered listening to any of your usual nonsense."

I perched at the foot of his bed, out of sneezing distance, I hoped. "It's not nonsense. As we speak, the aliens are in orbit, preparing to invade. Why won't you believe me? It's not like you don't believe in aliens. Zorbon the Decider is an alien."

"Yes, but that's different," he said, drawing breath like Darth Vader with a chest infection.

I felt my hackles rise. "So *your* alien—who I've never met—is perfectly real. It's just that you don't believe in *my* aliens."

Zack groaned. "This is Miss Dunham all over again. You see supervillains and aliens because you want to. Not because they're real. Because the only power you have is the power to make stuff up."

That didn't sound like much of a superpower. Even Arm-Fall-Off-Boy's power was better than that.

"I mean, come on," he continued, coughing into his fist. "Cara finally kisses me, and you try to explain it away by inventing some ridiculous *War of the Worlds* scenario."

"Great," I said, throwing up my hands, "so *now* you get it." I was mad. How was my alien invasion any more ridiculous than what he'd faced in the mall? "Where do you think the giant robot came from? Best Buy?" I shook my head. "Don't you see—it was part of the aliens' nefarious plan."

"The aliens who all look like Miss Dunham?"

"Yes."

"Who sent a robot that looks like Cara to kiss me?"

"Yes. Though technically she kissed Star Guy. Not you." I had a horrible thought. "You're not planning to, y'know, *reveal* yourself to her, are you?"

Zack propped himself up on his elbows. "Just to be clear, Luke, you mean take off my mask, right?"

Strange thing to say. What else could I possibly mean?

He rescued Sir Isaac from the fruit bowl and set him down carefully on the floor. "When we kissed there was this incredibly bright light, and I felt a tingling sensation all through my body." A faraway look came into his eye. "Do you think that happens every time?"

I think he'd drunk too much Theraflu. "Uh, or maybe it happened because you were shot by an alien super-weapon, you goon."

Under normal circumstances I could expect a thump for the "goon" comment, but he just gave me this dreamy look and said, "Why am I asking you? It's not like you know anything about girls and stuff."

The sue-dunham's distraction plan had proved even more effective than the Overlord could have hoped. All Zack cared about was kissing Cara.

I had one last move. Maybe Zack wouldn't believe me, but he had to believe his own eyes. I reached into my pocket. "If there aren't aliens, then what do you make of this?" In my palm lay the sue-dunham remote control.

"Now *that* looks like it came from Best Buy," he said. "A TV remote. So what?"

"Yes, but this one can turn your voice off and on,

and open security doors, and who knows what else. It's advanced alien technology. Allow me to demonstrate."

Before I could continue, Zack raised a hand. "I don't doubt it can do what you say. But is it alien tech, or is it one of Christopher Talbot's crazy inventions, hmm?" He fixed me with a hard stare. "Why were you at the mall with him?"

I could have told him about my team-up with the former supervillain. About how he'd faced down the alien commando like a Jedi knight. But I'd already wasted too much time trying to convince him about the invasion. "It's complicated," I said, and slid off the bed. Even if the flu hadn't blunted Zack's superpowers, it was obvious that he was going to be of no help. My path was clear, and Star Guy wasn't on it.

As I reached the door, he sat up. Our conversation had tired him out, but when he spoke his voice was firm.

"Luke, you have to listen to me. You can't trust Christopher Talbot. He's dangerous."

"Yeah, he's dangerous." I shrugged. "But at least *he* believes me."

I left my brother to stew and headed downstairs. Somewhere an alien clock was ticking. There was no telling how much time remained before the invasion, and I had a lot to do. The absence of sue-dunham attack ships over town gave me a sliver of hope.

I decided to call the army, hoping that they had some secret weapon designed for this eventuality. But the only number I could find was for the local VFW office. They couldn't put me through to the experimental weapons division, but they did sign me up for a sponsored bike ride to raise money for veterans.

I put down the phone. What was the point? If I couldn't even convince my own brother that the invasion was real, I had no chance with some general, even if I could get through to one. It was my responsibility now. Somehow, I had to come up with a plan to defeat the invaders and save Earth—without Star Guy, without the military, without my friends. The fate of the world rested on my shoulders. It felt a lot heavier than I ever imagined.

FLASH! AH-AAAHH!

I didn't have the first idea about how to overcome the sue-dunham. They'd been successfully conquering planets for centuries; I'd barely made it through half a semester of junior high.

I paused next to the hall table, my eye caught by one of the framed photographs that always sat there. The photo was in a slightly different spot than usual, which is the only reason I noticed it. Someone else must have picked it up for a better look. It's one that Mom took of Dad, Zack, and me. We're at the beach. I'm four years old, and I'm sitting on Dad's shoulders, holding an ice-cream cone smothered in chocolate sauce. We look happy (a lot happier than we would be ten seconds later, when I got spooked by a seagull and accidentally deposited the ice cream on Dad's head).

I studied the smiling seven-year-old Zack in his

Superman T-shirt, and I remembered that he only wore it to please Dad. Of course we had no idea then who Zack was going to turn into. Even now, I still had no idea who I'd become, and the thought scared me. So much about growing up seemed dark and uncertain. It hit me that if the aliens invaded, I wouldn't have to worry about any of that stuff. My future would be decided for me. Along with everyone else on the planet, I'd be a mindless zombie sitting in front of a screen. But would that be so bad? Everything would stay the same. I'd never have to be scared about growing up again.

"Luke, are you OK? *Luke?*" A gentle touch on my arm broke my trance. Mom stood over me with a concerned look. She'd been saying my name over and over, but I hadn't heard her. She placed a hand against my forehead.

"Well, you don't have a temperature," she said, relieved. "We wouldn't want you missing the wedding too."

"No," I mumbled. "That would be awful."

She wanted a little mom-to-second-son chat, so we went into the kitchen. I sat at the table while she set out a bowl of disgustingly healthy snacks. Carrots? I mean, seriously, who in the history of the multiverse ever wanted to snack on carrots?

"It's your dad," she said, pulling out the chair opposite me. "He's been a bit down about everything lately."

Something about this conversation felt different from our usual ones. Most of the time Mom made it perfectly clear that she was in charge. And as much as I disliked being told what to do, there was comfort in knowing that Mom or Dad always had the answers. But now her voice was filled with uncertainty. The safety net suddenly looked like it was hanging by a thread.

"He'll get another job, won't he?" I asked, for the first time unsure of the answer.

"Of course he will." She fiddled with the button on her collar. "But right now . . . well, he feels . . . what's the word?" She thought for a moment. "Powerless."

I knew the feeling.

"He's been watching old TV clips on the computer again," she said. "All day. Would you go in there and sit with your dad, Luke? You could give him a hug, if you felt so inclined."

I didn't have time for this—I had to save the world. But it wasn't as if I had any idea how. I could spare a few minutes. I nodded.

A minute later I tipped open the living room door. The curtains were drawn, the only light the glare from the computer. It flickered across my dad's face as he lounged in front of the screen, a party-size bag of M&M's open on his lap.

He glanced up as I came in and then patted the seat. I slid in beside him. Playing on-screen was an ancient black-and-white film.

"Flash Gordon," explained Dad. "The 1936 vintage. They don't make 'em like this anymore. Rocket ships held up by visible strings, garden lizards pretending to be dinosaurs, cliff-hangers with actual cliffs."

The current scene was set in a futuristic palace, represented by a shiny curtain and a throne that looked like it came from IKEA. A woman with curly white-blonde hair was talking to a bald man wearing a cloak with a pointy high collar, and a mustache and beard that were obviously stuck on. Baldy sat on the throne, stroking his fake beard.

"Who's he?" I asked.

"Emperor Ming the Merciless. The big bad."

"And her?"

"Dale Arden. Flash's main squeeze. Though if you ask me, Flash picked the wrong gal. Y'see her?" He pointed to another woman in the shot, wearing what looked like a sparkly bikini top and a tiara. "That's Princess Aura— she's Ming's daughter." He studied her. "I think your mom looks a bit like Princess Aura."

I couldn't see it myself, but Dad seemed pleased at the similarity.

"What has become of Flash Gordon?" demanded Dale Arden.

"You will never see the Earthman again," crowed Emperor Baldy. *"You are to be mine. I, Ming the Merciless, will take you as my bride this very day!"*

"Aaand she's fainted again," said Dad. "Quick, have an M&M. Every time Dale Arden faints, you have to eat one." He shoved the pack under my nose. "She faints a lot."

We sat side by side, crunching. "Why is she marrying him if she doesn't want to?" I asked.

"She has no choice," said Dad. "Ming's planning to use his Dehumanizer on her. It's a device to make her forget all about her true love, Flash Gordon."

I noticed Mom hovering at the door. Dad hadn't seen her.

"Did you use a Dehumanizer on Mom before you got married?"

"Naturally," said Dad. "A woman like that'd never agree to marry a man like me, not without an alien mind-control device."

I saw a smile appear on Mom's face.

"What powers does Flash Gordon have?" I asked Dad.

"Powers? None, unless you count his handsomeness. He's not technically a superhero. In the original comic strip he was a polo player from a fancy university."

I couldn't hide my surprise. "So he's just an ordinary person?"

"Well, yeah," said Dad, "apart from the polo

ponies and the two-hundred-and-fifty-thousand-dollar education."

An ordinary person who saves the earth. I'd never considered the possibility.

"But he can't do it alone—he has great friends and allies. Like Dale Arden, Dr. Zarkov, who's a brilliant scientist, and Prince Vultan of the Hawkmen." He patted my leg. "Now sit back and enjoy. We've got thirteen episodes of this, and then a sequel, and then we can move on to Buck Rogers."

Flash turned up. He'd been right about the strings showing. It was tempting to sit there with my dad and watch ancient space adventures until my eyeballs fell out of my face, but then I caught Mom's expression. She wasn't angry. She just looked sad. And in that instant I understood the true evil of the sue-dunham. Sitting in front of a screen all day, every day, might sound appealing—it could even be fun for a while—but the reality was, I didn't want to spend my life watching someone else have adventures.

I wanted my own.

"You have to turn it off," I said.

"I will," said Dad, with a longing glance at the screen. "Soon."

I laid a hand on top of his. "Ask yourself this: would Flash Gordon spend all of his time watching old TV shows?" I didn't wait for his answer. "No! He'd much rather be out there, soaring through the galaxy in an old laundry detergent bottle spray-painted silver, fighting for humanity, wearing infeasibly tight shorts." I paused. "Dad, put down the keyboard."

He glanced down as if noticing it for the first time and then slowly set it on the coffee table. Mom came softly into the room. The two of them looked at each other for a long time.

With a click the laptop entered sleep mode. The dark screen pulsed like a starless galaxy. A shudder went through my body.

I had an idea.

Half in a daze, I tripped out of the living room.

"Luke, are you OK?" asked Mom as I floated by. "What's going on with you today? I really hope you're not coming down with your brother's flu."

I barely heard her. Threads of ideas spun in my head. One by one I wove them into a single perfect plan. In fact, a plan not so much woven as *knitted*. I knew how to defeat the Overlord, but I couldn't do it alone.

It was time to activate S.C.A.R.F.

EMERGENCY PROTOCOL ALPHA

The statue of the winged boy tinkled into the pond in Serge's backyard. As soon as the plan came to me, I'd called Lara, made an excuse to my mom and dad, and headed straight to Serge's house. I had been making owl noises for fifteen minutes without a break when he finally came to the window. Thankfully, he was alone.

"You know I am forbidden from associating with you," said Serge, with a cautious glance over his shoulder. "You must depart."

The current situation went way beyond his *maman*'s ban on our friendship. I had to make him understand the gravity of our circumstances. "I'm activating S.C.A.R.F. emergency protocol Alpha," I said.

"You cannot," he breathed.

"I have to."

"No, I mean, you cannot . . . because we do not have

an emergency protocol. We did not even sign off on a logo."

"Perhaps not," I agreed. "But we were definitely going to have one, and now I'm activating it."

He paused and then nodded. "*Oui*, that makes sense." With that he reached for the window latch. "I shall be right down."

No one can refuse an emergency protocol Alpha. It's one of those things, like Obi-Wan Kenobi's ghost whispering instructions in your ear, or seeing a Bat-Signal displayed on the underside of a cloud, that you just don't ignore.

By the time we reached the tree house, I had brought Serge up to speed on everything that had happened since we'd gone our separate ways. I could tell from the way the corners of his mouth turned down in a pout that he keenly regretted missing out on my adventures, especially the bit where I'd escaped from the alien mother ship. He asked me to tell him about that again, and not to leave out a single detail. As I began the story a second time, I felt a warm glow envelop us. And it wasn't a heat ray. It felt good to be back with my best friend.

Lara was waiting in the tree house, alone. Christopher Talbot had not been invited. Although a temporary ally, he was not cleared for such a high-level S.C.A.R.F. meeting. Also, he had an appointment at the bank about a small business loan.

"*Bonjour*, Lara," said Serge, greeting her with his customary kiss on both cheeks. He made it look as natural as Spider-Man slinging a web.

"I wasn't sure you'd come," I said to her. "So now you believe me about the Cara-borg?"

Lara nodded. "At first I was sure the robot was merely a ligament of your imagination." I let that slide, and she went on. "But after the kiss at the mall, I knew you were telling the truth. The real Cara would never kiss Star Guy, not when she already has a boyfriend. That thing in my house is an evil cyborg impostor. No question. So let's talk about how we rescue my sister and save the world."

We sat in a circle to discuss the plan. Serge unwrapped a Snickers bar. I'd never been the head of a secret agency dedicated to fighting intergalactic invaders before, but I'd come prepared. I slid a patch over my right eye. Ideally, I would have preferred a black one, but CVS only stocked them in flesh color.

I reached for my backpack and drew out my trusty Martian Manhunter clipboard. "There is only one point of business on our agenda today." I turned the clipboard around to show them the headline, "Thwarting the

Imminent Alien Invasion." The others listened intently. "To recap, even though they have put Star Guy out of action, for some reason the aliens have not yet launched their main assault on Earth."

"Well, it's obvious why they're holding back, isn't it?" said Lara. "They fear me."

Serge choked on a mouthful of Snickers.

Was she kidding? She had to be kidding. I lifted my eye-patch and searched her face for an indication.

She wasn't kidding.

"In a manner of speaking," I said, "you're absolutely correct."

"She is?" said Serge. Lara glared at him.

"It took me ages before I understood what Zorbon the Decider was thinking when he gave you your particular power," I began. "Zack's were built specifically to take on a planet-killing asteroid. Yours seemed more suited to battling an evil dog trainer. But Zorbon knew what he was doing when he gave you such a lame superpower. It's the very lameness that's going to help defeat the aliens."

"OK, OK, I get it," she said. "But can you please stop calling my superpower lame?"

I agreed that I would. "We dismissed you, just as the aliens have. They don't consider you a threat, when in fact you're the proton torpedo headed right down their unshielded thermal exhaust port."

"I'm the what going where?"

"Never mind," I said. "It'll all make sense when we go through the plan."

"So how do we stop the invasion?" asked Lara.

"We don't," I said. "Hold off a massive aerial assault? Repel thousands of alien warriors in hand-to-hand combat? No way. We're just a bunch of kids. And even though one of us has a superpower, S.C.A.R.F. doesn't have the resources to fight off a cold, let alone defend the earth against a full-scale alien invasion." I could see that Lara and Serge were confused. Hadn't I invited them to the tree house expressly to hear my alien-defeating plan?

"We can't stop an invasion." I smiled. "But we can stop a TV show."

THE SHOW MUST GO OFF

The tree house door banged open, and curling brown and gold leaves skittered across the wooden floor, pushed by the eager wind. In its cold fingers I could feel the first chill of winter.

"Just the wind," I said, catching sight of my friends' troubled expressions. Darkness was falling, so I switched on the tree house's lights, which consisted of three battery-powered LEDs, each modeled on a different member of the Avengers. We huddled around the glowing figures of Iron Man, Thor, and the Hulk as I explained my strategy.

"When I was aboard the mother ship, the Overlord told me that the aliens' whole society is based on a reality TV show. They're only invading Earth so that they can transmit live pictures of it back to their home world. Which means if we can stop the sue-dunham from being able to broadcast the show . . ."

"Then they will have no reason to invade," finished Serge, his eyes wide as flying saucers.

"You want to turn off the aliens' TV?" said Lara dubiously. "*That's* your plan?"

I held up the alien remote control. "End the transmission, stop the invasion."

I looked around at my friends. In our hands lay the fate of humanity, while in my brother's hand was a snot-filled tissue.

I made a space on the floor, put down the alien remote, and unrolled a map of the school that I'd drawn myself.

"Does the alien ship really look like our school?" asked Lara.

"The sue-dunham wanted to make it as scary as possible," I explained.

"You don't like school, do you, Luke?"

I shrugged. "It's OK," I said.

"I'm scared too," said Lara.

That came as a surprise. "But what about all that stuff you told me about growing up? Being a superhero vet? You can't wait, you said."

"Sometimes I feel like that. But a lot of the time I'm *apprehenful*."

I think she meant *apprehensive* or possibly *fearful*. Usually when she tripped over a word, I wanted to correct her, but at that moment it just made me feel closer to her than I had for ages.

"I too have the fear," said Serge. "I believe Josh Khan may be on to me."

"*On* to you?" said Lara.

"Each time he visits my house, I wait until he is napping post-*déjeuner* in my armchair, and then with my *maman*'s tweezers I pluck out one of his nose hairs, causing him to leap up in acute but fleeting pain. It is a small victory, but it makes me feel better about myself. Thus far I have successfully passed blame for each assault on our cat."

"I didn't know you had a cat," I said.

"I do not," said Serge. "And I fear Josh Khan may also be coming to this realization."

This wasn't the time to concern ourselves with imaginary cats. I turned back to the map. "Our primary mission objective is the ICT department, here." I stabbed a finger at a section on the uppermost deck of the mother ship. "The Overlord showed me when she was explaining her plans for world domination. The invasion will be broadcast from this classroom."

Lara pored over the layout. "So, let's say somehow we manage to get aboard the mother ship, make it past all the guards, dodge the inevitable booby traps, and reach the heavily defended classroom without being caught. How do we knock out the transmission?"

"We need a mole aboard the mother ship," I said.

"You mean a deep-cover double agent?" said Serge.

"No," said Lara. "He means a small garden mammal with velvety fur." She paused. "I think I see where you're going with this." She picked up the plans to study them in closer detail.

"I am less clear on the role of the mole," said Serge.

I explained my thinking. "Moles are some of the best diggers in nature. A well-briefed mole, dropped in the right place, with instructions to burrow into the central control panel, would be able to use its powerful forelimbs to sever wires, demolish circuits, and generally wreck the aliens' capability to broadcast."

Lara lowered the plans. "And I think I know just the mole. They call him"—she narrowed her eyes—"the Wraith."

Serge and I looked at her.

"What?" she said. "So I know a mole with a nickname. Get over it."

"That is all very well," said Serge. "But how do we get aboard the mother ship in order to, as you say, insert the mole?"

"With this," I said, reaching into my backpack for the *Puny Earthlings!* game disc. "Just as soon as we figure out how to make it work. Or, I should say, as soon as Christopher Talbot figures it out."

"No way," Lara objected. "He can't be on our side. He's a villain."

"We need him," I said. "If anyone can work out how to use this disc to reverse the teleporter, it's the man who built the Tal-bots and the Mark Fourteen Sub-Orbital Super Suit."

"What about Zack?" said Lara. "Is he feeling any better? I've tried calling him on the telepathic line, but all I get is a squelchy sound."

"That would be his head cold," I said. "He's completely stuffed up. And his phlegm is currently mustard colored."

"Did you see that?" said Serge. "The alien remote control. It moved." He pointed. "There! It is doing it once again."

He was right. The buttons moved as if pressed by invisible fingers. Someone was operating the remote . . . remotely.

The infrared bulb pulsed, and a holographic screen appeared in the air. The ultrahigh-definition image displayed the back of a high black leather chair. It was so realistic that it appeared as if the chair was in the tree house.

"Quick," I whispered to Lara, "put on your mask."

Lara lowered the mask over her eyes just in time. From the screen came a creak of leather and a rapid sidestepping of feet, and then the chair spun around to reveal its occupant.

"Greetings, Luke Parker of Earth," said the Overlord, steepling her fingers. Her cold eyes surveyed the three of us. "So this is the mighty army you have assembled to foil my invasion. Impressive. Perhaps I should give up right now." From offscreen came a broadside of amused whistles.

"You don't scare us," I said, standing shoulder to shoulder with my friends. "We're S.C.A.R.F., a secret superhero organization dedicated to fighting evil wherever we find it. Serge, show her the logo."

"Ah, I would prefer not to," said Serge. "I am unhappy with the latest version."

The Overlord ignored us and beckoned with a hand. "Bring in the prisoner." Two more sue-dunham scurried into view. Held between them was the struggling figure of Cara.

"Let go of me, you monsters," she said, wriggling and kicking.

"Cara!" Lara called out. "Are you OK, sis?" She winced at her mistake. "*Sis*-picious. This looks highly suspicious."

Cara squinted at us out of the holographic projection. "Dark Flutter?"

"Uh, yeah," said Lara. "Hi." Thankfully, even after

Lara's slip of the tongue, her sister hadn't recognized her with her mask on. "Just want to make sure they're treating you according to the Amnesia Convention, citizen."

"Uh, I think it's called the Geneva Convention," said Cara. "And yeah, I'm OK. Thanks for asking, Dark Flutter." She spotted me. "Kid! You made it. So where's the cavalry? Star Guy's on his way. Right?"

"Well, Luke Parker," interrupted the Overlord, gleefully. "Do you want to tell her—or shall I?"

Cara gazed out hopefully. How was I going to break it to her? "About that. Yeah. The cavalry." I coughed. "You're looking at it."

Her face crumpled with disappointment.

"But I'm here," chirped Lara. "I'm part of the cavalry."

"Great," said Cara mournfully.

"It doesn't sound like you think it's great," grumbled Lara.

At a command from the Overlord, the guards dragged Cara off, still struggling and yelling some very rude words, two of which I hadn't heard before.

"We'll rescue you, Cara," I shouted after her. "I promise."

The Overlord laughed. "You can't win, Luke Parker of Earth. Someone always tries to outwit us, but it never works," gloated the Overlord. "Whatever you're planning, we've seen it before." She counted off on her fingers. "Building giant robots to defend your planet? Season ninety-two. Battleships? Season two hundred. Moving speech about love in the face of existential annihilation? Too many seasons to mention. Small nuclear device concealed in a stuffed toy animal? Season four hundred and six."

"Ah, *zut*," said Serge quietly.

"And see this?" She held up a thick paper file and riffled the pages. "Shielding maintenance schedule for the thermal exhaust ports." She dropped it with a thud. "Oh, and before you go trying to infect us with your sneaky Earth bacteria," she said, rolling up one sleeve of her tracksuit to present a fresh red lump on her bare upper arm, "we've all had our shots."

She leaned back in her chair, looking as relaxed as I felt panicked. "I think that about covers everything. Now, as per standard invasion procedure, the main assault will commence on a date resonant with the invadee's history. We find it adds to the drama. Thus we will take over your world on October twelfth." She paused for effect. "Independence Day!"

From offscreen the rest of the sue-dunham whistled their approval. I raised a finger of objection, and the Overlord silenced the horde.

"What?" she snapped.

"Uh, that's not Independence Day," I said. "Independence Day is July fourth."

"No, it's not." Irritated, she clicked her remote several times. A list of dates with brief encyclopedia entries scrolled through the air. "See. October twelfth. Equatorial Guinea's independence day. What *do* they teach you in Earth schools? If you ask me, it's a good thing you're being invaded."

October 12 was tomorrow. The same day as my cousin Jenny's wedding. She was going to be really annoyed.

"Keep watching the skies, Luke Parker." The Overlord smirked. "At prime time on the twelfth, tune in for the exciting conclusion of . . . *your world*." She shuffled her feet, and the chair began to turn away again. She paused. "One more thing. Almost forgot." She glanced out of the holographic screen. I followed her eyeline to the remote control. The infrared bulb blinked steadily. In the quiet of the tree house, I could hear a faint *bleep bleep bleep*. "As you earthlings say . . ." She raised her eyebrows. "Snap."

"Snap?" I said.

She frowned. "No, wait. Not *snap*. What was it again? Ah, yes." She smiled thinly. "Checkmate."

"Out!" I cried, pushing Lara and Serge ahead of me to the door. "It's a countdown! Get out!"

The three of us scrambled to the edge of the deck. There wasn't time for Lara to call for her birds. She threw herself onto the rope ladder and lowered herself in a couple of athletic moves. Serge went next, and I brought up the rear. A boom shattered the stillness of the afternoon, and a pulse of heat threw me down to the ground. Lifting my head out of the dirt, I craned my neck to look back.

The tree house was in flames.

The fire department arrived in time to prevent the fire from spreading, but the tree house was gone. When Mom and Dad saw the damage, they did that parent thing of being simultaneously relieved and utterly furious. In the end they accepted it wasn't my fault—I hadn't been playing with matches, or flamethrowers. The firemen put it down to a catastrophic failure of my Avengers lamp set. No one considered the possibility of an alien booby trap.

The remains of the tree house smoldered in the last of the evening's light. The sun dipped below the horizon, and the oak was a dark shape against the cold sky. Standing in the yard, I pulled my coat tightly around me. Never again would I set foot in my tree house. Even if we decided to rebuild, it wouldn't be the same. All the hours I'd spent there were already turning into memories. All the arguments with my brother, the homework I'd ignored, the plans I'd hatched—gone. Helpless, I'd watched the fire consume my favorite spot in the whole world.

"Now I know how Captain Kirk must have felt when the *Enterprise* self-destructed over the Genesis planet," I said.

Serge stood at my shoulder. "And when the *Enterprise* crashed in the Battle of Veridian Three."

I nodded. "And when the *Enterprise* was destroyed defending Narendra Three from the Romulans."

"And when the *Enterprise* was destroyed by the Tholians," said Serge.

We stood in silence, our breath white streamers in the cold air.

"The *Enterprise* gets blown up a lot, does it not?" said Serge.

There was no time to mourn our loss—we had an alien invasion to foil. "Come on," I said. "It's only a tree house." We turned for the house and made our way back into the warmth.

INDEPENDENCE DAY

"There. So handsome," said Mom, adjusting my collar for the billionth time. "So grown up."

"Mommm," I complained. I was in a suit. Not a space suit, which would have been much more useful, but a two-piece tuxedo from JCPenney.

It was the day of the wedding, Equatorial Guinea's independence—and the invasion of Earth. While the people of a small Central African republic prepared to celebrate the anniversary of their independence from Spain in 1968, and my cousin Jenny did whatever brides do before they walk down the aisle, they had no idea that hidden in orbit above us, alien invaders were making their own preparations.

There was a knock at the door, and Dad strolled into my bedroom. He took one look at me and began to stroke an invisible cat in his arms. I knew exactly what he wanted, but I wasn't in the mood.

"I'm not saying it," I said, folding my arms.

"Oh, come on," he said.

I gave in. "All right, all right." I cleared my throat and said, "Do you expect me to talk?"

Dad gave his invisible cat another stroke and tented one eyebrow. "No, Mr. Bond, I expect you to die."

"Happy now?" I said.

Dad beamed. "Look at you. Your first tux. I have to take a picture." He put down the invisible cat, pulled out his compact super-zoom, and began to snap away. "Act natural," he said, shoving the lens in my face. "Pretend I'm not even here."

My grumpiness resulted in part from being forced into the suit (not to mention the bow tie and pinchy new shoes), but mostly from my frustrating phone call with Christopher Talbot that morning. He'd given me a cell phone so that we could keep in close communication. I'd been asking my parents for one for ages, but as ever when I asked for anything cool, they ended up giving me shoes. I'd called Christopher Talbot shortly after dawn.

"Do you have any idea what time it is?" he'd said groggily.

"It's shortly after dawn," I'd replied. "Have you figured out how to make the teleporter work yet?"

"No, not yet."

"But you've had ages!"

"Listen, *matey*, we're talking about reverse-engineering some pretty wild alien technology."

"But we're running out of time, Christopher Talbot!" I'd worked out precisely how long we had. According to the Overlord, the invasion would commence at prime time. Prime time was when TV networks could expect their biggest audiences, and so that's when they broadcast their best shows. Which obviously meant *Doctor Who*. So that meant the invasion would start at 7:30 p.m.

"How long until we're operational?" I'd asked. "Realistically, if we're going to have enough time to stop the aliens, we have to get aboard the mother ship before the hors d'oeuvres."

"Don't you worry," he'd said. "I'll be ready."

"I hope so. We're all counting on you." I'd thought about that for a moment. "The whole world's counting on you."

"Yes, it is," mused Christopher Talbot, "isn't it?" And he'd hung up the phone.

Since it was going to be tricky for me to slip away from the wedding venue, the plan was for Christopher Talbot to rendezvous with me at the golf club with the teleporter. But would he be ready and waiting in the men's locker room with a fully working device? He'd better be, since we didn't have a backup plan for boarding the mother ship.

To my relief, Dad put away his camera. "Finally," I said. "So are we done here?"

"Not quite," he said. "Your outfit is missing one important detail. Here." He delved into a pocket of his own suit. "I have something for you."

I was hoping he'd continue the James Bond theme. "Is it a fountain pen with a concealed grappling hook?"

"No, son, it's—"

"An underwater jetpack?"

"Yes, Luke, that's what's in my pocket. An underwater jetpack."

Dad opened his hand to reveal a pair of silver cuff links, one shaped like Superman's shield, the other Batman's bat sign.

"Allow me," he said, reaching for my shirt cuff. "These things are tricky to put on by yourself." He slotted them in place one after the other.

"They're engraved," said Mom.

In the center of the Superman cuff link were the words "Here I Come . . ." I twisted my other wrist so that I could read what was on the bat sign: ". . . to Save the Day." I said thank you and was about to add that they were cool when Dad called them "snazzy," and that was the end of that.

Mom and Dad left to go and finish their own preparations. Meanwhile, I was under strict instructions to stay away from anything that might spill, splash, or otherwise mark my new clothes. I wasn't sure whether that included Zack and his projectile snot, but I decided to risk it. I had to speak to my brother.

Zack was asleep, his eyes gummed shut, his breath gurgling like a coffeemaker. I knew Mom had said he needed plenty of rest, but this was important. I shook him by the shoulder.

His eyes flicked open, and he shot up into a sitting position. "X-squared plus y-squared equals pl"

Typical. He even dreamed math. He squinted at me and grunted his displeasure. "What do *you* want?" he said, convulsed by a series of rapid-fire sneezes.

"Dad says Flash Gordon didn't have superpowers," I said, passing him the box of tissues, "but he saved the world, thanks to a good education and the help of his friends. Christopher Talbot isn't my friend, but he definitely is a mad scientist; Lara isn't Prince of the Hawkmen, but she is kind of Princess of Pigeons; and Serge has low blood sugar, which can make him faint, though not as much as Dale Arden."

Zack screwed up his face in an expression of bafflement. "What are you talking about?"

"I know you don't believe me about the alien invaders," I went on, "but it's true. And if we fail our mission, then it's going to be up to you, Zack. Flu or not, the world will need you. Oh, and if you happen to get your strength back in the next few hours, the mother ship is in orbit right above the town. You can't miss it. It looks like our school."

I could tell that he didn't buy a word of what I was saying. I turned to leave, and as I reached the door, a thought struck me. If things did go badly, then this might be my last conversation with my big brother. He was still sitting up, watching me with the same mystified expression. "I just want to say, you've turned into a good superhero, Zack. I mean, obviously you're no Superman or Batman. But I'd rate you as a solid Aquaman."

"Thanks?" said Zack.

I left him to bask in my excessive praise and returned to my bedroom. I fired off a text to Christopher Talbot, requesting an update on the teleporter's readiness. As I waited for a reply, Mom popped her head in the door. "Time to go. And feel free to tell me how lovely and elegant I look in my dress."

"Do I have to?"

Five minutes later the three of us jumped in the car and headed off along Moore Street. We hadn't gone far when we were stopped by a traffic jam. It looked like all the people had left their vehicles.

"What's going on?" said Dad.

"Maybe there's been an accident," I said, lowering my window and sticking my head out.

Everyone was looking up. I followed their gaze, and stifled a gasp.

"What on earth is that?" said Mom.

Ranged across the dreary afternoon sky in flaming letters a hundred feet tall were the words COMING SOON.

As we watched, the phrase faded out, to be replaced by a series of short scenes: a heat ray melting a city, hundreds of alien strike fighters spilling out of the belly of a mother ship; alien flags being raised over blasted state buildings. Each scene was accompanied by the same vibrating musical note, which sounded like BRAAAM!

The last scene faded, and the "Coming Soon" banner reappeared. Beneath it materialized the number 3:00, in equally giant burning numerals.

As I watched, the number changed.

2:59

The countdown had begun.

"Ah," said Dad, climbing back into the car. "Must be for the new episode of *Doctor Who*." He glanced at his watch and sighed. "We'll still be at the wedding. Don't worry, Luke, I TiVo'd it."

I mumbled thanks. But of course I knew it wasn't for *Doctor Who* at all. Those were clips from previous seasons of *The Show*.

It was a trailer for the end of the world.

I THEE DREAD

When we pulled into the golf club's parking lot fifteen minutes later, there was still no reply from Christopher Talbot. I jumped out of the car. The countdown burned far above me, visible for miles around. The trailer seemed to be on a loop, repeating every few minutes. Tearing my eyes away, I followed my mom and dad inside. A sign in the tartan-carpeted entrance hall welcomed guests to the wedding of Ms. Jenny Simpson and Mr. Marvin Malik.

"Never thought I'd see the day," muttered Mom.

My cousin Jenny and Marvin had been together for what seemed like forever, but always insisted it would be the end of the world before they got married. So the day after Earth narrowly missed extinction by the Nemesis asteroid, they booked the golf club. It struck me that if my mission failed, the end of the world might beat them to it this time.

I was desperate to get on with things, especially now that the aliens were broadcasting our forthcoming destruction. However, S.C.A.R.F. was firmly earthbound until Christopher Talbot sent me the signal.

In the meantime Mom made me mingle. My grandparents were at the wedding, which meant I had to suffer yet more endless cooing over my outfit. The only thing more annoying than all the attention was the number of times people asked me about Zack and said what a shame it was he couldn't be there. I let Grandma Maureen squeeze my cheek and call me her "scrumptious pumpkin" one last time, and then gave the oldies the slip. I headed off to find Serge.

I'd been allowed to bring one guest, so obviously I'd chosen my best friend. His *maman* permitting, he'd be waiting outside. As I approached the double doors, I spotted a girl in a dress standing next to a tall vase of flowers. I'd almost missed her, since the pattern on her dress blended perfectly with the pale pink flowers.

It was Lara. Until that moment I'd only ever seen her in jeans, a really bad Catwoman outfit, and her Dark Flutter costume. "You're wearing a dress," I said, unable to hide my surprise.

She wrinkled her nose. "Great eye, Sherlock."

I couldn't take my eyes off her. During one of Dad's previous YouTube binges, he had shown me a series of old TV commercials featuring monkeys wearing human clothes. Not that Lara reminded me of a monkey in a dress—just that seeing her in one was at least as startling.

"*Bonjour, mes amis,*" said Serge, sauntering up. He was also in a suit, but judging by how comfortable he looked, his didn't itch the way mine did. His bow tie hung loosely untied around his neck, but instead of appearing untidy, it made him seem relaxed and confident. My hand went to my own bow tie. It was a clip-on.

"Did you observe the giant burning countdown in the clouds?" he said.

"Kind of difficult to miss," said Lara.

"And yet still not as dazzling as you," said Serge.

"*Merci,* Serge," said Lara. "And you look good too. Very sharp."

"Ah, this old thing?" said Serge, smoothing the front of his jacket.

I'd never been to any occasion that required dressing up like this. Until today, I'd been to more alien mother ships than weddings.

Lara turned to me. "Both of you look very handsome."

I felt my cheeks flush, and my shirt collar was suddenly as tight as a noose. "Monkeys in dresses," I blurted.

The other two studied me with deep puzzlement.

"Lara, what are you doing here?" I said, attempting

to cover my outburst. "You should be in the men's locker room."

She scowled. "Yes, Luke, I am well aware that I was not officially invited to the wedding."

Something told me to change the subject. "Where's your mole?" I asked.

Lara unclipped the clasp of a tiny handbag, and a pink, pimply snout poked through the gap. "Gentlemen," she said, "meet . . . the Wraith."

The mole squeaked. "He wants to know which one is Star Guy," Lara translated. "I've told him a million times that Star Guy's not coming." With that she uttered a series of squeaks of her own, which I guessed explained this to the mole for the millionth and one time.

All everyone wants is to meet Star Guy. Even underground mammals. It's highly irritating.

As Lara conversed with her mole, Serge took me aside and in a whisper said, "I sense some tension between you and Lara. What is going on?"

"I have no idea," I said. "She *does* keep trying to get me alone to tell me something important. Only me—she doesn't want to speak to anyone else."

Serge raised an eyebrow.

"What d'you think that's about?" I said.

"It is perfectly clear to me, *mon ami*." He put a hand on my shoulder. "She has fallen for your charms."

My throat went dry. I looked across at Lara, chirping away at the Wraith. During the Nemesis adventure, I'd had to pretend she and I were going out, but that was purely for operational reasons. This was different. This was terrible. She wanted to be my girlfriend.

"Luke, are you feeling all right?" she said, glancing up.

"Ummm, finethankyouverymuch." My voice came out as squeaky as the Wraith's. I buried my head in my phone again. "Need to check my messages." Still nothing from Christopher Talbot. "He'll come through," I said, although even I was starting to wonder if he could make the alien teleporter work in time.

A voice piped up from behind me. "Well, if it isn't *Puke* Skywalker."

I spun around to see Josh Khan standing there in a suit two sizes too big for him. His bulky shoulders heaved with laughter. "Now *that's* funny."

"What are you doing here?" I stuttered.

Josh's index finger idled at the entrance to one nostril. "Hmm?"

"Why are you at my cousin's wedding?" I said.

"*Your* cousin?" said Josh. "Uh-uh, it's *my* cousin who's getting married." He stared hard, daring me to object.

"Oh, for goodness' sake," said Lara. "Obviously, your cousins are marrying *each other*."

Josh's glower gave way to a look of bored comprehension. Then he noticed Serge. "Steve! Steve-o! Steve-a-matic!" He clapped Serge several times on the back. "What are you doing here with this loser?" He thumbed at me.

I watched in outraged silence. I'd never met Josh at Jenny and Marvin's house, so that meant he couldn't be a close relative. However, that didn't change the inescapable fact. I waved a finger back and forth between us. "Does that mean we'll be . . . related?"

A terrible screeching filled the room. I clamped my hands over my ears. The sound wasn't just in the room; it was everywhere. I motioned to the others, and we went outside onto the putting green. It was as if someone was trying to tune the loudest radio in the galaxy. Finally, they landed on the station they were searching for, and a tune blasted out of the sky.

I recognized it instantly. "That's the Overlord's theme from *Puny Earthlings!*"

The tune ended, and the voice of the Alien Overlord boomed out in ultrahigh-fidelity You Are Surrounded Sound™.

"People of Earth, we come in peace."

There was a distant echo, as if her voice had traveled a long way, and I realized that the Overlord must be broadcasting to the whole planet. Right now the president having a hamburger in the White House would be listening, wondering what was going on. My mom and dad and everyone at my cousin Jenny's wedding had come outside and were listening too.

The Overlord chuckled. "Sorry, earthlings. We *never* come in peace. Prepare to *faint* at the terrifying mother ship hurtling toward you on an unstoppable path, *dread* the technologically superior fighter-bombers about to rain fiery doom on your population centers, *scream* at the simultaneous ground assault by an alien army wielding weaponry so far beyond your own it's like playing Ray-Guns versus Sticks." She lowered her voice to a whisper, like a late-night radio DJ. "It's the end of civilization as you know it."

"Must be some episode of *Doctor Who*," muttered Dad.

"What did you say?" asked Lara.

I shrugged. "I didn't say anything."

"Huh. Sounded like *beep-beep*."

Could it be? With a shaking hand I lifted my phone to check the display. There was a text message alert. I clicked on the envelope to see the words I'd been waiting for: READY 2 BEAM UP.

I turned to the others. "Mission is a go. We are green for teleportation."

YEAH, IT'S A DESSERT CART

We sprang into action. Lara collected the gym bag containing her Dark Flutter costume from where she'd stowed it behind the flowers. Serge's fingers were a blur as he expertly tied his bow tie. The three of us made our way quickly to the men's locker room.

We hurried past rows of polished wooden lockers to the far wall. Ranks of golf shoes poked from beneath low benches like the feet of an otherwise invisible army. There, at the end of the last bench, stood a pair of brown suede loafers. Unlike the rest, these shoes were filled. By Christopher Talbot.

Screwdriver in one hand, soldering iron in the other, eyes hidden behind protective goggles, he hunched over the guts of a video game console. Curling cables sprung from connectors, hooking up the dismantled console to various external devices. Among the random bits of apparatus, I recognized a keyboard and a car battery and, at the heart of the tangle of wires and circuit boards, the alien game-disc-that-was-really-a-teleporter. The whole contraption sat on what looked suspiciously like a dessert cart.

The soldering iron hissed, its white flame reflecting in the dark lenses of the goggles. Christopher Talbot snapped the flame off.

"There. Finished!" He pushed the goggles onto his forehead. "Impressive, hmm?" A satisfied smile played across his lips.

Lara voiced what I was thinking.

"There's no way that thing's teleporting anyone. It's just a bundle of wires and stuff."

His smile evaporated. "How typical of your generation. Just because something doesn't come in a fancy box with a fruit-based logo doesn't mean it's not cutting-edge technology." He wiped his hands with a cloth. "It'll work. Trust me."

I edged closer for a better look. Nestled among the seemingly random collection of bits and bobs was some kind of mysterious dome-shaped device in a small dish. I was about to poke it when Christopher Talbot flung out an arm.

"Don't touch that," he cried. "It's my bomb."

I froze in horror. We hadn't discussed anything about a bomb.

Serge studied the device with an expression of professional interest. "Ah, *oui*," he said, nodding. "I believe what we have here is a chocolate-covered ice-cream *bombe*." Serge was an expert on all things confectionery and patisserie.

Christopher Talbot's silence confirmed my initial suspicion. "Did you steal a dessert cart?" I said.

"No," he said flatly. "Pass me that spoon." Serge was closest. He handed it over; then Christopher Talbot broke the chocolate shell with a brisk rap and took a bite. "One minor technical hitch," he said through a mouthful of pilfered dessert. "I made a slight error in my power calculations." He tapped the car battery with the spoon. "This thing's not going to give us enough electrical juice to power the teleporter."

"How much more do we need?" I asked, looking around the locker room. "There must be an electrical socket in here."

Christopher Talbot shook his head. "It's going to take significantly more than that, I'm afraid. I'll have to use my superpower."

His electrical energy power was our most potent weapon. I'd been counting on him arriving on board the alien mother ship with a full charge. If he used it for the teleporter, it would be a whole hour before he'd be able to summon another blast. But there was no alternative. We had to get aboard that ship.

"Mmm, delicious." His spoon rang in the now-empty dish. He looked around at us. "Oh, my profound apologies. Did you want some?"

Lara squared up to him. "I want it on record," she said. "I don't like you. And what's more, I don't trust you." They were toe-to-toe. "Make one wrong move and you should know that I have a squirrel with your name on it."

"Uh, I think it's time to suit up," I said, pushing Lara's gym bag in between them to prevent further confrontation. She snatched it from me and went off to change.

"Very tense, isn't she?" said Christopher Talbot, but not before she was out of earshot.

"Hey, you guys," said a voice. "I've been looking everywhere for you."

Josh Khan stood at one end of the locker room.

"What are you doing in here?" he said, making his way toward us. "Did you hear that weird message? Voice sounded kind of like the one in *Puny Earthlings!*, don't you think?" As he drew closer he noticed Christopher Talbot, and then his eye fell on the dessert cart teleporter. "What is *that* thing?"

This was disastrous. How on earth was I going to explain away all of this? But before I could say anything, there was a swish of a cape and from out of the gloom strode Lara, wearing her superhero costume.

"Dark Flutter?" gasped Josh. "Is it really you?"

"What's he doing—" Lara caught herself. "Hi. Yes." She raised a palm in greeting. "It is I, Dark Flutter. How are you?" She cleared her throat. "I mean, who are you?"

"I'm Josh. It's short for Joshpal," he said, clasping one of her gloved hands and pumping it furiously. "I can't believe it's you. Everyone prefers Star Guy," he said, and Lara scowled. "But you're my favorite."

"I am?" said Lara.

"Of course. Animal powers are the coolest."

"Yes, they are, aren't they?" she said, pleased.

"Uh, Dark Flutter," I said, "we're running out of time. The mission clock is ticking. Let's go."

Josh stepped in front of me and began to prod a finger at my chest. "Hey, you can't order her around. She's Dark Flutter." He sneered. "You're nothing. You're just—"

"Commander Luke Parker," interrupted Lara coolly. "Leader of S.C.A.R.F., a secret superhero team on a do-or-die mission to save Earth from alien invaders."

Josh's lips moved, but no sound came out.

"Ready when you are, Commander," said Lara, snapping a salute.

"Very good," I said, thrilled at her timely words, and desperately trying to keep a lid on my delight at the effect they were having on Josh. "Initiate teleportation procedure, Christopher Talbot."

"Aye-aye, *Commander*," he replied. Electrical energy poured from his fingertips into the device. By the crackling light I watched Josh Khan's stunned expression.

"Dark Flutter," I said. "Do you have *the package?*"

She patted a small pouch hanging from her belt. "The Wraith is aboard, Commander."

With a whine, a green cone of light rose from the game disc, just as it had in Crystal Comics.

"I told you it would work," crowed Christopher Talbot. Suddenly, he grimaced and staggered into the bench. His superpower faltered. "Quickly, I don't know how long I can hold it open."

"OK, S.C.A.R.F.," I said, addressing the others, "we're going in."

Time was of the essence, but I couldn't resist taking one last shot. I turned to the slack-jawed Josh. "Y'know, I'd love to have you on the team, Josh, but I'm afraid Steve took the last spot." I gave him a sympathetic clap on the arm.

Serge waved to catch his attention. "Ah, Josh Khan, there is one thing I must tell you also," he said. "I do not have a cat."

Josh said nothing, just sat down heavily on the bench. And the look on his face? Now *that* was funny.

Grinning to myself, I followed the others and stepped into the teleporter.

26

IT'S NOT A BIG BLUE BRAIN

"Look out!" yelled Lara.

I had barely stepped from the teleporter at the other end when she grabbed my arm. A quick glance around at my surroundings confirmed that we were aboard the mother ship, but not where I expected to be. Instead of the gym, we had beamed onto another deck entirely. Rows of exhaust fans whirred as enormous ovens blasted hot air. Gigantic fridge-freezers ringed the room like the sculptures of a frost-free Stonehenge. The air was filled with the smell of school lunches. It was the kitchen.

Lara, Serge, and I were hemmed in by sue-dunham lunch ladies, each brandishing a different kitchen utensil.

"Careful," said Serge. "She's got a ladle."

The lead lunch lady swaggered before us, wielding her ladle. Beside her another rattled a set of measuring spoons. A sieve, a whisk, and a clicking pair of tongs completed the set.

Lara reached for a large bowl on the counter and threw its contents across the floor. Undercooked Brussels sprouts rolled like marbles in front of the advancing aliens. The sue-dunham lunch ladies went flying.

"Quickly!" shouted Lara, sprinting for the door.

My shoes scrabbled for grip on the linoleum as I hurried after her. "Great," I muttered. "Pinchy *and* slippery." I wondered how James Bond did it, carrying out all those missions in formal shoes.

From close behind us came more angry whistles as the aliens gave chase. We sped past long tables stacked with impossibly tall towers of cardboard boxes. There had to be thousands of them.

"Must be packed lunches for the invasion force," I said, panting.

A volley of apples thudded against the door frame as we hurtled out of the kitchen. We ducked down a corridor and doubled back, giving our pursuers the slip. Finding the relative safety of a storeroom, we paused to catch our breath and regroup. Only then did it hit me that we were a man down. "Where's Christopher Talbot?"

"Perhaps he was teleported somewhere else on the ship," said Serge.

Lara gave a snort. "I bet he never even got into the

teleporter. He's not exactly the bravest, is he? Do you really believe a man like that would willingly hurl himself into outer space to take on a bunch of evil aliens? I would say that he chickened out, but that would be an insult to some very daring poultry I know." She unbuttoned the small pouch hanging from her belt. The Wraith wriggled out and sat happily in her outstretched palm. "At least we haven't lost our secret weapon," she said, tickling him under the chin and making goo-goo noises. "Have we, Wraithy?"

I forced a smile. In truth I wasn't ecstatic about having to rely on any secret weapon that enjoyed being tickled.

Could she be right? Had Christopher Talbot abandoned us? I'd watched him face down an alien commando on Main Street, so I knew he could be brave, but it was true: most of the time his main tactic was to run away. To my surprise I wasn't angry. I felt sad for him. Once he'd dreamed of being a superhero, but now it seemed he didn't even have the courage to try.

Something else was bothering me. "The aliens all look like Miss Dunham because they probed my mind and picked the form that would scare *me* the most." Puzzled, I turned to Lara and Serge. "But why do they *still* look like her now that you're here?"

"She's pretty scary," confessed Lara.

"Ah, yes," said Serge. "I have faced nothing more

terrifying in my life than dodgeball with Miss Dunham."

At the door the Wraith wrinkled his pimply pink snout and squeaked.

"He says he detects no worm-sign," said Lara. "I think that means the coast is clear." She popped the mole back in his pouch, and we crept into the corridor. I quickly plotted a route to the ICT department situated on the top deck of the ship.

As we made our way through the mother ship, I reviewed our dire situation. My original plan had fallen to pieces as soon as we boarded without our most powerful team member. We were stretched thinner than a thin-crust pizza.

"We still have to hit the ICT classroom first," I said. "Once the Wraith does his stuff, the sue-dunham will have plenty to keep them busy. While they're dealing with the chaos, we'll rescue Cara."

I wished I felt as confident as I sounded. I was learning the hard way that plotting the downfall of a race of alien invaders from the comfort of your tree house didn't prepare you for the reality of creeping through a spooky spaceship surrounded by hostile life-forms.

"This way," I said, taking the lead. The walls of the corridor were lined with unsettling symbols. I didn't have to know the sue-dunham's language to understand from the vivid diagrams of flaming alien skulls, electrified bodies, and melting eyeballs that these were warning symbols. The science corridor lay before us.

"I don't like it," said Lara. "Where are the sentries? Why aren't alarms going off? They know we're on board."

There was a swishing sound behind us as a sue-dunham scientist in a hazardous-materials tracksuit plodded out of one of the labs. Before I knew what was happening, Lara had pushed Serge and me through the door of another classroom.

"That was close," she breathed, when we were safely on the other side.

I looked around. We were inside an alien laboratory. It was a lot like the labs at school, with a fume hood, rows of workbenches scarred by experimental mishaps, and the whiff of rotten eggs. But there were a few key differences. In our science lab hung a globe of the earth. The aliens' ceiling was strung with dozens of different planets—I guessed they were worlds the sue-dunham had conquered. And where our lab was brightly lit to avoid accidents, this one was as dim as a movie theater. It was also empty of scientists and silent except for the whir of an exhaust system and a low gurgling from a row of six glimmering tubes that stretched from floor to ceiling.

At one end of the lab were squares of blue light, a bank of touch screens that floated like lightning clouds. What was it about alien screens that they always hovered in midair? Maybe aliens were like my dad and not very good at screwing brackets into walls. We'd lost three TVs that way.

Lara crossed to the closest of the glowing tubes. Her face shone in its eerie light. "What do you think's inside?"

It was hard to see through the thick fluid swirling like creamy coffee inside the tube, but I was pretty confident I knew. "Almost certainly a giant blue brain," I said. "That's the sort of thing you're likely to find in a weird alien stasis pod."

"Or a tentacled horror," added Serge.

Lara took a step closer. "I don't think it's either of those things. In fact, it looks kind of familiar." She placed a palm against the outside of the tube.

We had to make it to the ICT classroom before prime time—in less than an hour and a half. I was about to tell Lara it was time to leave when I noticed a cell phone on one of the workbenches. And not an alien one. I picked it up and thumbed the home button. The phone sprang to life to reveal a grid of icons against a background image of a smiling girl and boy. It was Cara and Matthias.

"Hey, I've found your sister's phone," I said, turning to Lara, who was still standing next to the liquid-filled tube. "I wonder what it's doing in here."

As I puzzled over the question, there was a movement

in the tube, like the flick of a fish tail. Then from out of the dense swirl shot a hand. It thumped against the inside of the tube. A moment later a face emerged from the gloop, pressing itself to the glass.

With a gasp, Lara stumbled backward. "It's Cara! We have to get her out."

"Wait!" I shouted. "Look."

Something was moving in each of the other tubes. As we watched, the liquid drained off with a gurgle, like bathwater going down the drain. Now we could see into the clear-sided containers. Each held an identical Cara.

"It's not the real Cara," I said with growing horror. "They're Cara-borgs. This must be where the aliens build their evil robots."

The nearest one turned to find us in the gloom of the lab, her head swiveling like a doll's. Where the skin should have been tight across her cheekbone was instead exposed steel and one shining robot eye. She looked half-finished.

I knew what we were looking at. "These are proto-types," I said.

Lara glanced at the phone. "My sister's entire life is on that phone. They must have been using it to program the robots so they'd act just like her. Uh-oh."

"What?" I said.

"I know that look," said Lara, eyeing the nearest

Cara-borg. "She's not happy. We have to get out of here."

"Right behind you," I said. We hurried to the door as, with a whir, the containment tubes slid up into the ceiling.

"It is locked," said Serge, rattling the door handle.

I looked back to see the Cara-borgs step out of their tubes in perfect synchronicity, their big boots clumping down on the floor with a collective thud. All wore the same combination of jeans and a faded purple T-shirt from a field-based music festival.

I looked at Lara. "We have to get out of here. Fast."

"I'm on it." She set the Wraith on the floor and issued a series of commands. The mole scampered to the door and squeezed his body through the narrow gap at the base. "He needs one minute," said Lara.

"I do not think we have *une* minute," Serge said with a gulp.

The Cara-borgs marched toward us, an approaching storm of whirling mechanical limbs and sickly sweet perfume. I had to buy us some time. But how? Lara's words came back to me. *My sister's entire life is on that phone.*

Quickly I swiped through the lock screen and located the app I needed. I tapped PLAY and prodded the button on the side of the handset for maximum volume. I slid the phone across the floor. It came to rest at the feet of the approaching Cara-borgs.

From out of the speakers exploded the latest hit single from Billy Dark, Cara's favorite singer.

The descending boot of the first robot suddenly stopped. The Cara-borgs ground to a halt, as something deep in their programming responded to the music. One of them began to tap her toe. Puzzled, the others crowded around the tiny blaring phone. The hips of another started to sway. A cybernetic head bobbed. They couldn't stop themselves. The chorus kicked in, and as one, the Cara-borgs waved their arms in the air.

There was a click. The Wraith had unlocked the door from the other side. We dashed out into the corridor. I'd set the phone to play the whole Billy Dark album, which would probably keep the Cara-borgs busy for a while.

We raced around the next corner. I looked at my friends, and at the Wraith, peering from his pouch like a figurehead on the prow of a pirate ship, fur rippling. And for the first time I thought to myself, *We can do this. We can defeat the Overlord.*

"Are you humming the main theme to *Superman*, the movie released in 1978?" asked Serge.

I hadn't realized I was doing it out loud.

"No, do not stop," he said. "It is highly motivating." He added his voice to mine.

Lara stared at us both for a moment, and with a shrug began to hum along too.

MOLE TEAM SIX

"Luke," yelled Lara. "Incoming!"

We were pinned down in the Craft Design and Technology department, taking cover behind a makeshift barricade that we'd quickly assembled using a coffee table, a couple of blanket chests, and a highly impressive Ping-Pong table that we'd found in the woodworking classroom. Those weren't the only items we'd found—our sue-dunham attackers were in for a surprise.

A squad of ninja gym teachers rushed us, tumbling down the length of the corridor, their whistles shrieking.

"Don't fire until you see the whites of their sneakers," I said. "On my command . . . Now!"

As one we raised our weapons—a battery of glue guns—and unleashed a sticky barrage. Streams of hot glue coated the flip-flopping figures. Scrabbling to un-gum themselves, they lost their balance, careened into the barricade, and crashed to the floor.

I took a moment to straighten my bow tie and tug my white shirt cuffs so that an equal length poked from beneath the sleeves of my jacket. My cuff links glinted in the emergency lighting. "One more deck to go," I said, stepping over the groaning ninjas.

A camera in the ceiling swiveled to follow our progress, one of hundreds of electronic eyes that blinked from every nook and cranny of the mother ship. I knew the Overlord would be watching, and I had a feeling she wouldn't be enjoying this episode of her reality show.

She threw everything at us. Drones, laser trip mines, stink bombs. But nothing could stop us. Side by side, the three of us (and the Wraith) swept past waves of enemies, using expertise gained from years of reading comic books and summers spent watching superhero movies. It was S.C.A.R.F.'s time to shine.

"Regard," said Serge, pointing along the corridor.

We'd reached the Information and Communications Technology department. The main ICT classroom lay before us, flanked by nothing more threatening than a pair of potted plants.

"I don't like it," said Lara. "It's been too easy."

I stood bent over, clutching my knees, gasping for breath. "Are . . . you . . . kidding . . . me?" I looked at her. "Did you *see* that flaming skull-beast outside the Library Resource Center?" I glanced at Serge. "And by the way, great use of the drinking fountain there."

"*Merci*, Luke."

I turned back to Lara. "I mean, yes, we're here now, but I wouldn't exactly call our progress *smooth*."

The Wraith looked up at me and squeaked.

"What did he say?" I asked.

"It's tricky to translate," said Lara. "Closest in English would be 'Don't make a mountain out of a—'"

"Molehill?" I suggested.

Lara drew a sharp intake of breath. "That's offensive!"

I mumbled an apology. Moles were as tricky to understand as girls, although marginally more squeaky.

We'd done our best to sneak past the cameras on this deck, and I was pretty confident we'd avoided detection. "OK, the sue-dunham may well be planning something like Lara says, but at least we have the element of surprise."

Lara knocked on the classroom door.

"Lara!"

She winced. "Sorry, force of habit." With an apologetic shrug, she strode into the classroom.

At first glance it looked like a regular computer class, except that instead of rows of schoolchildren writing code to make an electromechanical claw pick up a LEGO, the desks were filled with sue-dunham operators wearing clumpy headphones, plotting to take over the earth. They sat stiffly in front of banks of floating monitors that displayed scenes from their invasion preparations. Fingers danced over screens as they swiftly edited footage before beaming it back to their home world and out to the conquered zombie audiences. A constant background noise of communications chatter filled the air. It was a smooth operation, practiced and perfected over the course of a thousand seasons.

From my position I could see several screens. On one an alien pilot, helmet tucked under her arm, gave an interview in front of her assault ship. Another displayed a ceremonial party of sue-dunham preparing an empty glass case in the Hall of Remotes, no doubt readying it for their next conquest: us.

At the front of the classroom, the Overlord sat in her command chair, overseeing the invasion on a giant tactical map that filled the wall. In one corner of the map, the countdown clicked toward zero hour. Less than thirty minutes remained.

The Overlord spotted us, and an expression of surprise and dismay slid across her face. She gripped the arms of her chair and slowly stood up. "You! But how did you . . . ? What about the . . . ? And the . . . ? Not to mention . . ."

She hadn't expected us to get this far. Her shields were down—nothing could stop us from completing our mission now. We marched toward her. It was strange, given that I was in the command room of an alien mother ship, but with Lara and Serge by my side, I'd never felt safer.

"It's over, Overlord," I said. "You're *canceled.*" *Now that's a quip,* I thought to myself.

"No, stay back! Keep away from me." She slapped a button on the arm of the chair, activating a communicator, and in a shaky voice said into it, "Abort the invasion! Prepare my escape shuttle immediately!"

This was awesome. We'd won! I wanted my moment of triumph to stretch out forever.

But that's the problem with triumphs: they only come in moments.

The Overlord lifted her head, and a snigger burst from her lips. "I'm sorry, I can't keep this up any longer." Her shoulders heaved with laughter.

I was confused. What was so funny? We'd vanquished all of her best henchmen and scared her into abandoning the invasion.

Hadn't we?

The giant map rippled and dissolved, revealing another section of the classroom behind it that until this moment had been hidden from sight. Rows of seats stretched into the distance, each occupied by a sue-dunham. They began to clap.

"What is this?" I asked over the applause. "What's going on?"

"Sadly, I cannot take credit for the idea," said the Overlord. "No, that must go to a mind even more devious than mine. So it is with great pleasure that I introduce this season's special guest star." A spotlight picked out a figure ambling along the aisle that divided the seated audience. "Mr. Christopher Talbot!"

"What a shocker," said Lara.

Christopher Talbot strolled through the audience, acknowledging their applause, shaking hands. He arrived at the command chair where we were gathered.

"What about our fragile alliance?" I whispered.

"I warned you not to trust me," he said.

"But you don't have to do this," I implored him. "You can be the hero. You've got a superpower. You're the Energizer!"

"Ah, yes, my nickel hydride charge," he said bitterly. "I worked it out. I possess the power equivalent of thirty-six golf cart batteries from 1990. Hardly Superman, is it?" He looked me in the eye. "I want you to know, Luke, it's nothing personal. It *is* with Chase, however." He tapped the command chair, and the Overlord looked up. "You will remember to vaporize the local branch, won't you?"

"Chase?" I said. "The bank?"

"Wouldn't give me that small business loan I needed," he explained. "I can't even afford the lease on my comic book store anymore. I'm going to have to close up shop. Not that it matters now. Thanks to my new friends here, I shall soon be the supreme ruler of Bavaria!"

"You're a traitor to the human race," spat Lara.

"Perhaps, but one who will shortly have all the *zwetschgenkuchen* he can eat." He paused. "It's a short-crust pie—"

"Covered with pitted *zwetschge*," I finished sadly.

"You remember," he said, and I was sure I detected a note of regret. I was angry and confused. I'd expected the double cross, but not until we'd defeated the sue-dunham together. "How could you do this?"

"It was very simple," he said. "Remember the commando on Main Street?" I nodded dumbly. "I was out-gunned. I knew I couldn't win, so I played the old 'take me to your leader' card. Or, in this case, conference-call me with your leader. You see, once you'd informed me that the invasion was a TV show, I had a proposition I wanted to put to the alien high command."

The Overlord interrupted. "And what a great pitch. Trust me, I should know. I've heard 'em all." She gave Christopher Talbot a salute, and turned to me. "Your former associate persuaded me to delay the takeover of Earth just long enough to give you time to round up your plucky friends and mount a do-or-die mission to thwart my invasion."

That made no sense. "But why? What could you possibly gain?"

A smile wriggled onto the Overlord's lips. "Agents of S.C.A.R.F.," she said, sweeping an arm toward the seated aliens. "Filmed *live* in front of a studio audience." More applause rolled out like waves. "And may I say, you were terrific." She clicked her remote control, and one of the floating screens appeared.

A recording began to play. It showed me, Lara, and Serge battling our way through the mother ship. The footage was slickly edited, and scored with music that somehow made us look foolish instead of heroic. The studio audience bellowed with laughter. We looked like real chumps.

The multitude of cameras that lined the alien vessel had caught every humiliating second of our ridiculous adventure, from every angle. What at the time had felt to me like a life-or-death mission was revealed to be a series of comedy sketches.

And we were the punch line.

"Remarkable performances," said the Overlord,

studying the film. "Such commitment to the role. You truly believe you're going to save the world. Of course, that's what makes it so *funny*."

"No," I mumbled. "This can't be happening." But it was. The feeling I'd had deep in my bones that we were invincible popped like a soap bubble.

"And that's just the preview," said the Overlord. "Wait till you see the finished film. *Sidesplitting*. I'm planning to show it to the defeated people of Earth, immediately after the invasion. They'll need a laugh." She leaned toward me. "Especially after all the pain and destruction I am about to unleash on your lovely blue planet." With that, she signaled to the guards. "Take them away."

"Not so fast." Lara stepped forward. "While you were distracted by all that gloating, I was executing our master plan." Cupping her hands to her mouth, she squeaked three times. I recognized the accent.

It was Mole.

"Right now," said Lara, "the Wraith is burrowing into your master control desk, ripping apart your fiber-optic ca—"

The Overlord flopped back into her chair, raised a palm to her mouth, and affected a bored yawn.

Lara bristled at the interruption. "Hey, I'm explaining how we just defeated you here."

The Overlord pointed over Lara's head. We all turned

to look. One of the sue-dunham operators held a small box with a tiny barred window on one side. The Wraith peered out, his paws wrapped around the bars.

"Burrowing mammals," said the Overlord. "Season four hundred and twelve." Her lip curled into a snarl. "As I was saying, *take them away.*"

PLANET EARTH IS BLUE, AND THERE'S NOTHING I CAN DO

The Overlord had barely finished issuing her order when an alarm began to blare.

One of the sue-dunham operators glanced up from what looked like some kind of radar display. She blew a series of anxious whistles.

The Overlord quickly rose to her feet. "What do you mean Star Guy is approaching?"

The radar operator gestured to a fast-moving blip on her display.

The Overlord raised a fist. "Open fire. *All* weapons!"

You might think after a command like that, there would be a whole lot of exciting laser-gun noises and the boom of photon torpedoes. In reality, it was pretty boring. We all twiddled our thumbs and looked around as various automated weapon systems attempted to down my brother in the silent vacuum of space.

Another of the sue-dunham whistled an update.

"In the air lock? He can't be!" said the Overlord. "Send a detachment of guards to—"

But she was too late. The classroom door burst off its hinges as Star Guy flew inside. He landed in what was now his usual fashion, one knee resting on the floor, cape fluttering behind him, head bent.

There was an excited squeak from the imprisoned Wraith. I didn't need a translation to understand that the mole was thrilled at the arrival of Earth's superhero savior. He wasn't the only one.

Zack slowly lifted his masked face. "Step . . . step . . ." he stuttered. He seemed to be struggling for breath.

The Overlord's alarm gave way to an expression of doubt, and she motioned to her guards. Warily, they took a pace toward my brother.

"Step . . . y'know, away from them," said Zack, waving a droopy finger at us. "Or feel the full might of Sta . . . ACHOO!" His forehead was slick with sweat, and his nose dripped like a faucet after my dad's tried to fix it. "I need to lie down." He flopped onto the floor and, shivering, pulled his cape around him like a blanket. "All that flying really took it out of me," he moaned. "Has anyone got some Theraflu?"

Star Guy wasn't saving the world today.

Scarcely had a smile reached the corners of the Overlord's mouth when the classroom resounded with a terrible creak of straining metal, and the deck of the mother ship tilted alarmingly.

The command chair, which was on wheels, rolled across the floor, rapidly picking up speed before crashing into a cluster of guards, causing one of them to drop the Wraith. Already off balance, they fell like bowling pins. The alien audience tipped out of their seats with a collective yell, while the Overlord and Christopher Talbot sprawled on the floor in a heap like a pair of tangled shoelaces. With a cry, the four of us pitched across the room.

"What's happening?" asked Lara, clinging to a desk.

"My guess is someone's tampering with the ship's stabilizers," I said, hanging on beside her.

"But who?" said Serge.

"Who cares!" This was our chance to escape. "Come on, help me with Zack," I said. Serge and I each took an arm and headed for the door.

Lara grabbed the Wraith's prison cage. "Right behind you."

As we hauled Zack off, he lifted his head and looked around blearily. "Oh, this is bad. The alien mother ship looks to me *exactly* like an ICT classroom." He groaned. "I must be sicker than I thought."

I was getting used to my new shoes and managed to keep my balance on the listing deck as we stumbled out into the corridor.

A lone figure blocked our path. A bandanna obscured the lower half of her face, and her hair was tied up in an efficient ponytail. Slung across her back was what appeared to be a bow improvised from a length of plastic pipe and a taut wire, and tied around her waist was a belt filled with arrows fashioned from plumbing materials and some kind of alien chicken feathers. She moved almost silently on sneakers wrapped in strips of cloth.

Beside me I heard Lara gasp with recognition.

"Cara?" I ventured. The last time I'd seen her, she was the sue-dunham's prisoner. Somehow she had escaped. Gone was the girl next door, and in her place now stood a fierce warrior.

Zack was in the throes of a fever, but even through his confusion he recognized his dream girl. I could tell because behind his mask he was making that stupid drooling face.

"Careful," said Serge. "How do we know she is not another Cara-borg?"

Cara pulled down her bandanna and fixed her gaze on Zack. "Star Guy," she breathed. "I knew you'd come." She took a step toward him. "I could kiss you!" She paused. "But I won't, of course, because I have a boyfriend."

"It's definitely the real Cara," whispered Lara happily.

Zack let out a sigh of disappointment.

I gestured to the tilting deck. "You did this?"

Cara nodded curtly. With a whir of compensating thrusters, the ship began to level out. "But it won't be long before they're shipshape again," said Cara. "Then this place will be crawling with search parties. Follow me." She led us along corridors I didn't know existed, taking us on clever shortcuts through classrooms, confident in every step. It was clear that school held no fears for Cara.

As we hurried to keep up with her, I turned to Zack. "So you saw the alien trailer?" He shook his head. "Then you heard the Overlord's message?"

He looked puzzled. "What are you talking about? I didn't see anything, and my ears are so full of orange gunk, everything sounds like it's twenty thousand leagues underwater."

It was my turn to be confused. "So what are you doing here?"

"Tylenol. But I can't take any more for another four hours."

"Not *how*—I want to know *why* you came. I didn't think you believed my story about the invasion."

"I didn't. Not until today in my bedroom." Sweat poured down his face. He looked terrible. "Just before you left, you compared me to Aquaman."

"So?"

"You gave me a compliment, Luke." He swallowed. "I

knew it really had to be the end of the world."

We reached our destination in the art department a few minutes later.

"We'll be safe in here," Cara said, holding open the door to the art storeroom. "The aliens don't know about this place."

We squeezed in among shelves filled with art supplies. I was just thinking that the storeroom felt even smaller than I remembered when Cara marched to the back wall and lifted it to one side, revealing a hidden compartment.

The wall was fake; several large squares of cardboard had been stuck together and painted over to look uncannily like a shelf laden with paints and art paper.

"You did this?" I asked.

"We're doing trompe l'oeil with Miss Chapleo this semester," Cara explained. She surveyed her work with a critical eye. "Though I'm not happy with the jam jars."

Serge nodded in sympathy. "It is the transparent quality of the glass that makes them difficult to capture."

More than her artistic skills, I was intrigued at Cara's transformation from ordinary teenage girl to Green Arrow. "Last time I saw you, you were a prisoner," I said. "What happened?"

She unhooked the bow from her back, swung it over one shoulder, and leaned on the end. "As soon as I found out Star Guy wasn't flying to my rescue, I decided to take matters into my own hands and rescue myself. It hasn't been easy. Escaping from detention, finding a place to hole up, designing and implementing a false wall, fashioning a weapon from everyday items." She ran a hand over one feathered arrow. "Although the hardest part was catching the chickens."

For the first time I had an inkling of what my brother saw in this girl. I felt an inexplicable urge to show her my comic collection.

Cara clapped me on the back. "You came back for me, kid, just like you promised. *And* with Star Guy."

"Hello? I'm here too," Lara piped up, raising a hand like she was in class. "Dark Flutter to the rescue."

"Oh, yeah," said Cara. "Didn't see you there, Dark Flutter."

Lara gave a huff of irritation.

"And may I express my eternal gratitude also," said Serge. "Thank you for swooping in to save us."

"I can swoop too," said Lara quietly.

"We don't have much time," I said. "What's the plan?"

"Well, I've raided the command bridge a few times, messed with their flight controls, hit the kitchens too—put salt in their pudding. They didn't like that. But it's all been low-level disruption. Until now." Cara grinned.

"Now that you're here, Star Guy, we can take down this mother ship."

Zack stirred briefly from his fever. "You're amazing," he cooed to Cara. "*Ah-may-zing*. And not at all robot-y."

"Is he OK?" said Cara.

"He has a cold," I explained. "It's made him lose all his superpowers."

"A cold did that?"

"An *evil alien* cold," I said, seeing the disappointment in her face.

"So you're not here to foil the invasion?" she said, addressing Zack.

"The Invasion? The inva—? Yes! Of course." He slapped a fist into his palm. "Those Martians don't know what's about to hit them. Martians. Martians. Martians. Martians. Y'know, if you repeat it enough, it loses all meaning. Meaning. Meaning. Meaning. Meaning." Suddenly, his eyes widened and he croaked, "Nemesis is coming!"

"It's been," I said with a sigh.

"Oh." He gave a great exhausted puff and sat down heavily on the floor.

I could see the dismay in Cara's face as it hit home: Star Guy might be here, but he was missing in action. I looked around at my friends' downcast faces. We were out of ideas and out of time.

Lara rooted through the shelves. "Here, take one of these," she said, holding out a tin of pencils and flipping open the lid. "Faber-Castell 9000 Graphite 2B. Ideal for sketching, note-taking, and brainstorming plans to save the world." As we each took a pencil, she shuffled a flip chart into the center of the room and flicked the pad to a fresh page. "We're going back to the drawing board. Thoughts?"

There was the whir of an electric sharpener as Serge honed the point of his pencil. "My apologies, but I cannot think with a blunt instrument."

Could we come up with another brilliant scheme before the aliens launched their invasion? The future seemed hopeless. Ours, mankind's. Hundreds of miles below us, my mom and dad and grandparents were at my cousin Jenny's wedding, unaware that they were a best man's speech away from the end of the world.

As I thought about my family, I fiddled with the cuff links Dad had given me. My finger traced the words engraved on their surface. Perhaps if I rubbed hard enough, a genie would pop out and grant me three wishes.

The motor of the electric sharpener cut off. "Ah, *zut*," said Serge. "It would appear that my 2B is not to be. The battery, she has died."

I squeaked like a mole.

"What is it?" asked Cara.

"We just got our first wish," I replied, taking the pencil sharpener from Serge and holding it up. Its surface shone under the harsh fluorescent ceiling lights. "I have a plan."

"I knew you'd come up with one." Lara beamed. "You always do."

"*Oui*, you are like a man with an attack of the hiccups," said Serge, nodding enthusiastically. "Except that the hiccups are plans. So, share with us this new hiccup."

They all looked at me expectantly. I hadn't felt this much pressure since basketball with Miss Dunham.

"Uh, well, it's not exactly a *new* plan," I said.

"Tried and tested." Serge glowed. "Even better."

"Actually, it's the same plan that we started with. More or less."

The Wraith poked his head from Lara's pouch and squeaked. "He says, 'Have you already forgotten that the aliens' computer systems are mole-proofed?'"

"I said more or less. Less mole. And more . . ." I hesitated. They really weren't going to like it. I took a deep breath.

"More . . . Christopher Talbot."

TO SAVE THE DAY

I stood back and let the others disagree loudly with my newish plan. They really didn't like the idea of Christopher Talbot being involved, and who could blame them? I still couldn't get over his betrayal. After all that hopping around deciding whether he wanted to be a superhero or supervillain, he had once and for all revealed his true colors: Penguin black. Joker purple. Doctor Doom green. And yet there was a tiny part of me that couldn't believe he had gone all the way to the dark side. Even if *he* believed it.

I called for order, and the others fell silent.

"Like it or not, our former enemy—"

"And *current* enemy," interrupted Lara.

I ignored her. "He is the only one left with a super-power capable of bringing down the sue-dunham." I drew a circle on the flip chart and swiftly sketched a couple of continents. "Christopher Talbot is Earth's last hope."

I explained exactly why we needed him, and one by one, they reluctantly agreed that while far from the ideal choice, he was the only one we had.

With a single purpose, we set to work. Everyone had his or her role to play—apart from Zack, whose contribution was limited to sweating on the floor. I looked around me and saw not a ragtag bunch of kids way out of their depth who really should have tried harder to get through to someone in the army, but a cool superhero team on a last-ditch mission. This was how I'd pictured S.C.A.R.F.

"The Wraith has volunteered to locate Christopher Talbot," Lara said. The mole squeaked his agreement. "He says he's able to sniff out a two-inch worm from a range of three hundred feet, so finding a worm the size of Christopher Talbot will be a piece of mud. I think mud is like cake for him."

We decided to split our forces. Serge and I would go with the Wraith while the others prepared for the escape part of the plan. Before we went our separate ways, Lara took me aside.

"Luke, what makes you think you can talk him into this?"

I knew the answer, but I didn't want to tell her. She would be horrified, and might never look at me the same way again.

Why would Christopher Talbot listen to me? Because we shared a brain.

Not in the giant-brain-in-a-tank-with-electrodes sense of sharing. What we had was a deep understanding. I'd always known it. From the first time we'd met in his duplex mansion, to when I'd faced the villainous Quintessence in his volcano comic book store, I'd had a hunch that we were similar. But our connection had finally become clear to me as I was playing *Puny Earthlings!*, as I'd gleefully plotted the downfall of Star Guy and Dark Flutter. I shivered with a mixture of horror and pleasure as I remembered the dizzying sensations. I was angry. I was unstoppable. I was *evil*. A game controller was the only thing that separated me from becoming Christopher Talbot.

In the end I didn't have to answer Lara's question. The Wraith squeaked his eagerness to get on with the hunt and scurried out. With a cry of good luck to the others, Serge and I dashed after him, leaving the relative safety of the art room behind us.

"Your *maman* worried I was leading you astray," I said to Serge as we trailed after the disappearing mole. "I wonder what she'd make of me leading you here."

"I have the confession," said Serge. "When my *maman* told me I could no longer see you, a part of me was relieved. I did not want to get into any more trouble at school," he explained, his voice catching. "To be known as one of the weird kids. It is difficult enough to fit in when you are so . . ."

"French?" I suggested.

"I was going to say *young*. We are summer babies, you and I, which puts us among the youngest in the class. It is a hard prospect. We are minnows in a sea where hormones swim like great white sharks. Have you seen the size of some of our classmates? And I suspect that Timothy Benson may already be shaving. So when school began, I believed that to survive I must forge new alliances."

I was gripped by a feeling of cold dread. "You were going to leave me behind?"

"No. I mean . . . How can I say? Per'aps there was a moment . . ." He sighed. "I panicked. I see that now. Can you forgive me?"

"Always," I answered. I couldn't imagine a universe in which Serge and I weren't best friends.

We made our way along the back alleys of the school, as Cara had shown us, avoiding patrols, sidestepping the sweep of surveillance cameras. The sue-dunham were too busy with final invasion preparations to notice us slipping through the ship.

The Wraith bounded ahead, coming to a halt outside a door. He raised his nose, sniffed, and then squeaked excitedly. I'd heard enough Mole to understand: he had tracked down our human worm.

"He's in the faculty room," I said, reaching for the door handle.

"It is forbidden," whispered Serge. "Students are not allowed in the faculty room under any circumstances. It is the unbreakable rule."

"Like the Prime Directive in *Star Trek*," I said.

"Precisely," said Serge.

"Which Captain Kirk is *always* breaking," I reminded him. I eased the door open and slipped inside.

My breath caught in my throat. The faculty room was a palace of marble and gold, the warm air filled with heady aromas. A great crystal chandelier hung from the ceiling, casting glossy light across the floor, which twinkled with a coating of what looked like crushed diamonds. Plump sofas made from the hides of endangered animals herded around the watering hole of a gently splashing fountain. I had to shield my eyes from the dazzling display. I breathed in the exotic scents of ambergris and camphor (I only knew what they were because of two candles on a coffee table labeled "Ambergris" and "Camphor," from the JCPenney Exotic line).

"So it is true," breathed Serge.

There had always been rumors among the students

about the unparalleled luxury of the faculty room. Now we were seeing it for ourselves.

I lowered my hand from my squinting eyes. Before me sat Christopher Talbot, stretched out on a plush leather armchair with a half-eaten box of chocolates. He wore a fluffy white bathrobe, his hair wrapped turban-style in a towel. He held a paperback novel in one hand, while the other was halfway to his open mouth, an orange cream clutched between his fingers. He froze in surprise.

With an electric hum, the chair inclined to an upright position. "Stay back! I warn you," he said, one chocolaty finger extending toward a control panel set into the arm of the chair. "I only have to push this button and a squad of guards will . . . Oh no, wait, not this button. That's the one for the massage. *This* button summons the guards."

"Push it," I said. He looked surprised. "But if you do, you'll never know what I was about to offer you."

He sneered. "What could you possibly offer me? Look around you. I have everything I want here. Big floating TV, mini-fridge, chair that goes up and down, the new iPhone. I'm on top of the world."

"But what about the world? Don't you care about what happens to the rest of us? What about your nephew? Your sister?"

"We're not close."

"Your mom and dad?"

He shook his head. "They passed away. A long time ago."

"I'm sorry," I said. And I was, truly. "But is this what they'd have wanted for you?"

"I know what you're doing, Luke. Trying to appeal to my better nature. Only problem is, I don't have one. Not anymore. Sure, when I was your age, all I wanted was to save the world. But then the world treated me badly. Now it's my turn." He sighed and stared into the distance. "You grow up hoping you'll become someone great, someone special. But then one day you look around at your empty comic book store and your Single-Serving Lean Cuisine Sesame Chicken, and you realize it isn't going to happen. But then, what's this—one last chance? And yes, placing all your hopes and aspirations into a shady deal with an alien race intent on world domination wouldn't be your first choice. But it's all you've got." His finger hovered over the controls. "Now, which was the guard button again?"

"What if this isn't your last chance?" I said. "What if—"

"Two last chances?" He scoffed. "Nobody gets two."

"He is, of course, correct," said Serge. "Technically it would move the existing last chance to the position of second-to-last chance. So then *this* would be the actual last chance."

"Forget it," said Christopher Talbot flatly. "There is nothing you can say to change my mind."

I was gambling that I could say exactly that. This wasn't like betting on cards with gummy bears; the fate of the entire human race rested on the next words out of my mouth. I took a deep breath.

"I have a time machine."

His finger drew back from the button. "No, you don't. That's ridiculous. What are you talking about?"

"I can take you back. To that time when you dreamed of becoming a superhero, when it was still a possibility. The time machine, it's in here." I showed him my clenched fist. "Give me your hand." I took a step closer.

He hesitated. Then curiosity got the better of him and slowly he reached out. I held out my fist and opened my fingers. There was a clinking sound as my cuff links fell into his palm.

Of course, I didn't have an actual time machine. But if I had judged Christopher Talbot correctly, these would have a similar effect. If I could become him, I was betting I could take him back to a time when he was like me.

The light from the chandelier rolled off their gleaming surfaces as he read the inscription. "Here I come." His voice wobbled. "To save the day." He looked up at me with a face full of confusion. And a glimmer of hope. On the outside he was still a tired, middle-aged man, but in his eyes I glimpsed the spark of the eleven-year-old boy he'd once been.

I took his hand and gently closed his fingers around the cuff links.

"Last chance."

SHOWTIME!

"First wave, commence launch in ten Earth minutes," boomed the Overlord's voice over the school's public address system. "And remember, I want to see impressive aerial formations, wanton destruction, and lots of screaming earthlings. OK, troops—it's showtime!"

The mother ship was a hive of activity. Or maybe that should be a nest. Or perhaps an underwater cave. I had yet to observe any of the sue-dunham in their true hideous form, so it was hard to say whether they were insect-, bird-, or octopus-based. Whatever they were, they were really busy, so it was quite easy for us to keep out of their way and spy on their preparations.

Of course, I'd seen plenty of aliens invade Earth in films and comics. But until you've been on board a mother ship in the run-up to zero hour, you have no idea of the amount of work that goes into it. Mobilizing all those assault ships and ground troops and hover-tanks takes attention to detail and lots of patience. The line for the bathroom alone stretched three times around the flight deck.

I couldn't help but notice that the aliens had decided to keep their current human skin. Even they couldn't come up with a form scarier than Miss Dunham. Hundreds of gym teachers in battle armor and flight suits mustered in the assembly hall for their final orders. When they hit our town, the real Miss Dunham was in for quite a shock.

"You're making the right choice," I whispered to Christopher Talbot as we snuck past a guard post. "The aliens would have double-crossed you. You'd never get what they promised. All they care about are viewing figures; they're planning to turn all of us into mindless TV-watching zombies."

"I know," he said, as we shuffled around the corner. "As well as Bavaria, they offered me a spin-off show." He snagged the sleeve of his bathrobe on a tack stuck to a bulletin board. There hadn't been time for him to change into regular clothes, but he had insisted on blow-drying his hair.

We dropped down outside the entrance to the gym. As arranged, the others were waiting for us. However much I tried, I couldn't shake my mistrust of Christopher

Talbot. I was hoping Zack had recovered enough to take over the role of savior of mankind.

My brother leaned against the bulkhead, letting out small moans, a cold compress laid across his feverish forehead.

My disappointment must have been obvious, because Cara said, "Actually, I think he's feeling a bit better."

I turned to Zack. "*Are* you?" If he was, then maybe his superpowers were coming back. I had to be sure. "I'm thinking of a number. Can you use your telepathic powers to tell me what it is?"

He narrowed his eyes in concentration. And then suddenly widened them. "Armadillo!"

Oh well. We still had Christopher Talbot. The rest of the S.C.A.R.F. team surrounded him with suspicious expressions.

"What are you looking at?" he said, backing away. "I'm on your side." His voice dropped to a mumble. "Again."

Lara folded her arms and scowled. "Sure, you're with us—until you get a better offer."

He looked hurt, which was pretty funny, given that he flip-flopped more than a pair of strappy beach shoes.

"How's the teleport situation?" I quizzed Cara.

"Taken care of," she replied with a smile, stepping

aside from the gym's open doorway. Inside I could see three sue-dunham tied up with jump ropes next to the pommel horse. "Our escape route is ready."

We didn't need it yet. I crossed my fingers and hoped there'd be an Earth to teleport back to.

The ship-wide address system shook once more. *"Commence invasion in five Earth minutes,"* announced the Overlord.

"That's our cue," I said, setting the timer on my phone for five minutes. "This way." We turned from the gym and set off toward our key objective. As we rounded the final corner, we skidded to a stop. Between us and our destination stood a familiar figure.

"It's . . ." began Lara.

"The Cara-borg," I breathed.

Zack looked even more confused than usual. He shifted his gaze from the Cara-borg to the real Cara and back again. His voice quavered as the terrible realization hit him like a smacker on the lips, and in a quiet voice he said, "I kissed an evil robot."

The Cara-borg brushed a strand of hair out of her face and smiled. "Nobody's perfect."

The real Cara stepped forward, slipped her bow from her back, and nocked an arrow. "She's mine."

"Hello, Cara," said the Cara-borg. "I have enjoyed living your life. I believe the earthling expression is 'walking in your shoes.' Which I have done too. I particularly like those wedge heels you think your mom doesn't know about. Though, small confession—I did rip that denim skirt of yours."

The real Cara tightened her bow. "The one from H&M or the one from Urban Outfitters? Y'know what, doesn't matter. So, who else have you been kissing?"

"Oh, you mean that hunky boyfriend of yours?" The Cara-borg made a face. "Not my type."

The real Cara gave an offended gasp. "What do you mean? He's handsome and gentle and smart and very tall."

"People can be too tall," said Zack.

The Cara-borg's hand blurred as she produced a silver remote control, a more elegant version of the clunky style I'd seen in the hands of the aliens. Weapons drawn, the two Caras began to circle one another.

"You know you're never getting off this ship," said the Cara-borg. "But don't worry, you needn't agonize about saying good-bye to your precious boyfriend. I already did that for you."

"What are you talking about?"

The Cara-borg smiled. "I dumped him."

The real Cara let out an anguished cry and leaped at the Cara-borg.

"Move out," I said to the others. If we were to have

any chance of defeating the sue-dunham, we had to go now. I figured the real Cara could take care of herself.

"But this is going to be epic!" complained Christopher Talbot. "I already missed the giant robot battle."

"On the double, people." I motioned to the others, and we slipped past, the first clash of combat ringing out behind us. "Agents of S.C.A.R.F., it's now or never."

THE ENERGIZER

"Two Earth minutes to launch," declared the Overlord over the public address system. *"First positions, please."*

"What are we doing *here?*" asked Christopher Talbot, surveying the rows of glass cases that lined the school entrance foyer. He shivered and retied his bathrobe more tightly. I hadn't noticed how cold it was the last time I'd visited. "Your plan is to turn off the alien broadcast, yes? Well, genius, all the important buttons are three decks above us in the ICT classroom."

"This is the aliens' trophy room," I said, steering him to the nearest case.

He inspected the contents of the case, then looked around. "Are these all . . . ?"

I nodded. "Remote controls from every planet they've conquered. Hundreds of them." We came to the heart of my plan. "Link all of them together and you create a massive infrared blast. One powerful enough to turn off the aliens' TV signal and stop the broadcast."

Christopher Talbot's brow creased in thought, and then a small smile appeared on his lips. "You know," he said, "that might actually work."

"There's just one thing." I removed the glass lid and lifted out the remote inside. I pulled off the back cover and showed him the empty compartment. "No batteries."

A look of understanding slid across his face like the sun rising. I didn't need to say any more. Like Superman, sent to Earth for a reason; like Batman, driven by his demons to save Gotham City, at last Christopher Talbot understood his purpose. He straightened and puffed out his chest. "This looks like a job for . . . the Energizer."

"I thought he was the Quintessence," whispered Serge.

Christopher Talbot moved wordlessly to the center of the room and, with a great grasping motion like he was pulling down the sky, summoned his superpower.

Electricity crackled from his fingertips. He stuck out one hand, and a jagged bolt reached through the nearest glass case to touch the remote control inside. Instantly, the device flew up, shattering the glass and settling into a midair hover. Its power button glowed like an eye opening.

With a cry that tingled to the distant ceiling, Christopher Talbot unleashed the full power of thirty-six golf cart batteries from 1990. The lightning charge leaped from case to case, ripping through the room. And one by one the remote controls sprang to life. Could a TV remote be alive? Looking around, it seemed to me as if an army of the defeated had stirred from their slumber and, sensing a chance to take revenge on their conquerors, risen with a single purpose. They smashed their glass prisons and whirled through the air in what at first appeared to be crazy orbits. I ducked as a pulsing remote shot narrowly over my head.

At the center of the spinning chaos, Christopher Talbot stood tall, directing the air traffic with grand orchestral gestures. And then at last I saw that all of the TV remotes were gradually forming into a grand fleet of handheld devices.

"Luke!" he yelled. "You and your friends have to leave."

"We will," I said. "As soon as you shut down the broadcast."

He guided the last handful of stray remotes into the main cluster. "No. I have to stay here," he said. "To make sure it works."

That wasn't the plan. "S.C.A.R.F. doesn't leave anyone behind."

He laughed. "I was never officially made a member of your superhero team, remember?" He glanced at the others. "I'm not sure I would have gotten in on a vote."

I started to say that I would have voted for him when he cut me off. "The comic store. I want you to have it." I didn't understand. What was he talking about?

"You'll find the deeds under my futon. Between the pages of *Uncanny X-Men*, issue one hundred and thirty-six."

It was a gesture of friendship, and yet I felt an unexpected rush of anger, as if he'd betrayed me all over again. As if he'd known even before setting foot in the Hall of Remotes that he wouldn't be leaving, and had kept it a secret from me.

"I got you into this," I said. "I'll get you out. I'll come up with a plan. I always do."

He shook his head. "Not this time."

"One Earth minute," declared the Overlord.

I felt the anger surge again. But now I understood where it came from. Frustration. I'd barely begun to know this Christopher Talbot—and I wanted to know more. Now I'd never get the chance. I couldn't do anything to save him.

He looked at me with a faraway expression. "I've seen an asteroid on fire at the edge of Earth's atmosphere. I've beamed up in a teleporter. I've held alien invaders at bay with my superpower. Not bad for a boy who stayed in his hometown." The remote control armada was complete. He guided the devices into a firing position. Hundreds of standby lights blinked their readiness. Christopher Talbot smiled. "Good-bye, Luke." And then his expression hardened. "Now *run*."

He flared his fingers and began to discharge every last amp of his battery power.

A thousand remotes fired.

Infrared is invisible to the human eye, but this fleet was assembled from devices acquired from strange and distant galaxies where perhaps our laws of physics didn't hold true. Which explained why I was watching a searing pillar of energy shoot from the remotes and tear through the ceiling. The blast rocked the room, throwing me across the floor, knocking the wind from my body. Zack, Serge, and Lara helped me to my feet. Lara had to shout to be heard over the deafening scream of power.

"Let's go!"

As Christopher Talbot continued to power the beam, the overhead lights flickered wildly. At the door I paused to look back. My eyes must have been playing tricks on me, because in the strobing light that fell across his figure, I could have sworn that I saw not a man but a boy. A boy with superpowers flowing from his fingertips.

That was my last sight of him, before Lara hauled me through the doorway.

We hustled along the corridor toward the gym. Cara was waiting for us.

"What happened to the Cara-borg?" asked Lara, as we took our positions at the teleporter.

"She turned out to be really nice, actually," said Cara.

"We had a great chat about academic options for next year. I said I'm taking Italian, and she said she's taking over the world."

Lara pouted, realizing her sister was pulling her leg. "*So* funny."

Cara gave a grim smile. "Let's just say she won't be borrowing any more of my clothes." She cast an eye over the group. "Where's Christopher Talbot?"

I shook my head. I tried to say that he wasn't coming, but the words lodged in my throat. Tears pricked my eyes, and I turned my head away so that they wouldn't see.

The Overlord's voice rumbled over the ship's address system. *"Begin the invasion on my command. We go live in . . . WHAT?!"*

There was a great whine from deep within the bowels of the mother ship, and it lurched like a little kid pushed on the playground.

"What's happening? Report!" In her confusion, the Overlord must have left her microphone on, because we could hear the chaos in the ICT classroom. There were whistles of dismay from the operators. *"What do you mean, someone's trying to turn it off?"* the Overlord demanded. *"The Show has never gone off. Keep transmitting or—AAGH!"*

The mother ship bucked again, and this time all the lights went out. A second later the emergency lights kicked in, bathing the gym in a hellish red glow. A frantic alarm sounded. And then, nearby, another. I could hear more in the distance. It felt as if the ship itself was freaking out.

"I think *everything* is shutting down," said Serge.

It was true. Our feet lifted off the deck as the artificial gravity quit. We floated for a second or two before it restarted and we thudded down again. If the ship's systems continued to fail at this rate, it wouldn't be long before everything went off-line, including the teleports.

I checked the controls. The power supply was weak and erratic, but the touch screen responded. We were still in business, but just barely. I tapped one of the disc icons, and the transporter beam activated. "OK, let's get out of here." One by one we vaulted into the light. I insisted on leaving last. When it was my turn, the Overlord's voice intruded once again.

"The Show *must go on! This can't be . . . the end?"* She let out a great howl of pain. *"Star Guy!"* she roared. *"This is your doing!"*

Typical, I thought, just as the teleporter whisked me away. *He always gets the credit.*

NORMAL SERVICE WILL RESUME SHORTLY

We beamed back to the men's locker room to find the clubhouse silent and empty. The wedding party was gathered outside on the putting green. I could see too that the road outside the club was filled with people and lights. A TV news camera crew broadcasted live from the scene. Frozen to the spot, all eyes were locked on the night sky. The light had been fading when we left; now it was properly dark. Prime time was here.

High above us, colored lights pulsed on the other side of a thin cloud layer. A monstrous shape parted the clouds. The shining mother ship hurtled down out of the darkness. I could feel the air throb with the shock wave of its passage through the atmosphere. With the ship's internal systems shutting down, its cloaking device had gone haywire. One moment it looked like our school, the next it settled into its real form, a hulking space battleship that made an Imperial Star Destroyer look like a rowboat. More lights in the sky. A pair of F-22 Raptors scrambled by the Air Force roared past on an intercept course. The giant craft ignored them as if they were a couple of insects. It looked unstoppable. The ship blew through the fiery hundred-foot-tall timer, which continued its relentless countdown.

Had Christopher Talbot's sacrifice been in vain?

There were murmurs from the wedding guests. Some of them had just noticed the appearance of Star Guy in their midst. Beside me, my exhausted brother heard them through his fever. They wanted him to do something. He lifted his head and peered up at the fast-approaching ship.

"You can't," I said. "You're not up to it."

He gave me a weak smile. "Luke, I have to."

Before I knew what was happening, he had sprung from the putting green and streaked into the sky. I could tell he was still under the weather, as his trajectory was a bit wobbly.

Millions of tons of battle-hardened mother ship bore down on his tiny figure. But just as it looked as if a collision was inevitable, the ship came to a rapid and complete standstill. Zack was visible against the ship's underside, lit up by its wildly blinking lights. The count-down reached three seconds.

Zack, his force field pulsing, wound up to deliver a

blast with his telekinetic superpower. I could feel the crowd around me tense.

Suddenly, there was a sound like a great big sigh, and the mother ship dwindled to a single point of light.

And vanished.

There was a long pause, and then a great cheer went up from the wedding guests.

Zack bobbed up and down in the now empty sky, illuminated by the light cast from the giant burning countdown. It had stopped with two seconds left to run.

"What just happened?"

It was Zack's voice in my head. He'd decided to reestablish our telepathic link. He might have been puzzled at what we'd just witnessed. But I knew.

Christopher Talbot had switched the sue-dunham . . . off.

The world's media went bonkers speculating about what happened that day. Some said that we'd witnessed the climax of a secret alien war the government had been waging without the knowledge of the general population. A surprising number of others were sure it was a mass hallucination brought on by artificial additives in chips. There were even a few who claimed it was a publicity campaign for Lab Rat Games' *Puny Earthlings!*

There was one thing that they could all agree on: Star Guy had saved the world. Again.

As much as it bugged me that my brother was receiving all the recognition, I was more upset at the thought of Christopher Talbot being overlooked. No one would ever know about his heroism. Except for S.C.A.R.F. And that didn't seem fair.

The fumigators left, and school resumed on a damp Monday in October. There was only one topic of conversation in the cafeteria; every table was abuzz with chatter about the recent UFO sighting. All but one. In the only quiet corner sat Serge, Lara, and me.

"He has a sister," I said. "She should know the truth about what happened."

"What will you say to her?" asked Lara.

I thought back to the last time I'd seen Christopher Talbot, in the Hall of Remotes. There was only one thing I could say: "Your brother was a superhero."

There was also the matter of the comic book store. It didn't seem fair that he'd left it to me when he had family of his own. Then I discovered that it wasn't like he'd left me something valuable. The rent was three months overdue, and the bank was about to take all of the store's stock. I figured his sister wasn't missing out on anything.

When school finished, I found Dad waiting at the gates. He didn't usually come to meet me, but since losing his job he'd invented new ways to fill his day. We strolled home through the park together.

"How was school?" he asked.

Things had definitely improved. Now that Josh Khan knew I was friends with Dark Flutter, he had stopped picking on me. But despite overcoming the alien menace, I still found school overwhelming, and there was this knot in my stomach that wouldn't go away. I think Dad could tell.

"What you've got to remember is that all you see of people is what's on the outside," he said.

"Like their masks and capes?"

"Yeah. I suppose, in a way, everyone looks like a superhero from the outside. Like they've got life figured out. But inside, trust me, they're all a bundle of insecurities, all worried about the same things. *What do I do now? Am I doing it right? Will they laugh at me?*"

"*Is my superpower a bit lame?*"

"Exactly."

My dad was no Yoda, but sometimes he came up with useful advice like this. There was something I wanted to ask him. I'd been thinking about Christopher Talbot a lot, and I needed answers. "Good and evil," I said. "It's kind of like a seesaw, isn't it?"

"Uh, I'm not sure I follow . . ."

"Well, when you're young it's really simple: there are

goodies and baddies, right? But when you grow up, you find out that sometimes goodies can go bad, and baddies can become good again, even right at the end."

"That's called redemption."

"So, does redemption make you feel good, even if you've been evil for a long time?"

"I think that's the idea."

I hoped so. I hoped that Christopher Talbot's redemption made him feel happy at the end.

The conversation turned to the UFO. Dad rattled on about it with as much excitement as any of the kids at school. He might be ancient, but he was still a fanboy at heart. That got me thinking.

"Dad," I began, as we swung past the duck pond, "have you ever thought about opening a comic book store?"

Zack bounced back to full health, which meant that in the unlikely event of the aliens returning, Star Guy would be ready to rumble. And this time he swore he wouldn't fall for any robot girl distraction. I knew he was sincere, because I could tell when he was lying. Like when he learned that Matthias and Cara weren't getting back together, and Zack said that was a real shame, what with Matthias being such a nice guy. Well, that was a big fat fib.

More importantly, Mom and Dad returned my Xbox. Now, you might think that almost bringing about the end of the world by playing *Puny Earthlings!* would count as some dreadful learning moment, and that in an act of newfound maturity I would have refused the gift. But you'd be wrong. I'd just be more careful in the future. Anyway, I didn't have as much time to play video games, not with my new S.C.A.R.F. commitments.

After witnessing firsthand how Serge and I performed aboard the mother ship, Zack and Lara agreed to let us help them with their future superhero exploits. S.C.A.R.F. was well and truly activated.

THE END?

And then there was Miss Dunham. She held true to her word with the punishment she'd chosen for Serge and me following our unfortunate misunderstanding in the gym. In our future lay a great deal of running around the track and rope-climbing. I tried to look on the bright side. Hadn't I said that I wanted to get in shape in time for the next threat to the world? Well, this was like having a personal trainer for the apocalypse.

The first session was set for the end of the very next school day. I decided to arrive early, to show my good attitude (and hopefully get out early too).

I changed into my PE clothes and made my way into the gym (which was now thankfully free from invading mold). The door clicked shut behind me.

"Luke Parker. Well, well, well." Miss Dunham eyed me from the center of the multipurpose court. I couldn't help staring at her—it was like being face-to-face with the Overlord all over again. The gym was empty. We were the only people there. She stood bouncing a basketball without looking at it, which was highly impressive. "Where's your partner in crime?"

I told her that he'd be along in a minute. I didn't mention that he was meeting the school's resident smuggler, Fred "Long John" Lobb, to acquire contraband. As part of a new health kick, some of Serge's favorite chocolate bars had been banned from school premises. But there wasn't a healthy eating campaign in the world that could get between him and a Kit Kat.

"We'll start without him," said Miss Dunham. "Something tells me that you were the ringleader anyway. Fetch a couple of mats from the storeroom," she ordered. "We'll warm up."

Still bouncing her basketball, she watched me as I crossed to the storeroom and opened the door. I reached for the light switch.

Harsh fluorescent light spilled across ranks of hockey sticks, crash pads, scoreboards, mini-trampolines—and a figure tied to a chair. I let out a gasp.

Jump ropes bound her ankles and were wrapped around her chest. She squirmed in vain, her cries for help muffled by a gag fashioned from a pair of sports socks.

It was Miss Dunham.

My first thought was to free her. My second was that

the noise of the bouncing basketball had stopped. Miss Dunham's eyes widened in fright as she stared past my shoulder.

I spun around only to find myself looking up into the face of the other Miss Dunham. Except, of course, it wasn't her at all.

My gym teacher was an alien overlord.

She fixed me with cold lizard eyes. "*The Show* is over. My crew and my command ship are gone. I was lucky to escape. And I know now it was *you* who brought an end to a thousand years of uninterrupted viewing pleasure. Not Star Guy, not the little girl with the furry animals, not that annoying girl with the bow. Not even that double-triple-crosser Christopher Talbot. *You* were the ringleader."

I tried to swallow, but my throat was dry. "I prefer 'leader of S.C.A.R.F.,'" I croaked.

She began to work her jaw like she was chewing a particularly sticky toffee. There was a terrible cracking sound as bone joints popped and tendons stretched. Her tracksuit bulged, and then two gelatinous orange tentacles tore through the material beneath her armpits. They swayed like king cobras. Her jaw wiggled and opened wider than humanly possible, until it gaped like the maw of some creature from a nightmare. Rows of sharp teeth shone from a mouth big enough to swallow me whole.

Behind me the real Miss Dunham's screams were muffled by her gag.

The Overlord's voice rumbled from the black pit of her mouth. "Once you asked me if we came to Earth to gather food." Her breath was hot and sour-smelling. "We did not." A long tongue darted out and caressed her stretched lips. "But I shall make an exception for you."

I glanced past her shoulder. I'd never make it across the court to the door before she caught me. The fire exit was just as far away. And there was no other way out through the storeroom.

I was trapped. And she looked hungry.

"Zack!" I shouted in my head. "I'm in trouble." I hoped he could hear me, but I had a horrible feeling he wasn't close by. I vaguely recalled him mentioning some math field trip.

A flash of light caught my eye, and I glanced up to see the sun reflecting off the glass ceiling. A skylight window was open. It wasn't as if I had any other option.

The Overlord lunged. I ducked and at the same time grabbed a hockey stick. Dropping to one knee as the real Miss Dunham had demonstrated to us in class, I swept the alien's legs out from under her. She crashed to the floor, and I sprinted to the foot of the climbing rope.

It rose above me like Mount Everest. I'd never managed to make it to the top before. Today would be a good day to change that.

I reached as high up the rope as I could and began to climb.

"There will be no escape this time, Luke Parker of Earth." The Overlord hauled herself to her feet and limped toward the wall. At least my hockey shot had slowed her down.

I was halfway to the top. I struggled on, desperately inching my way up toward safety. From above came an unexpectedly soft sound. At the window perched a cooing pigeon. The Overlord let out a roar, and with a squawk of alarm, the bird flew off.

I glanced down. The Overlord had reached the rope. Using a combination of arms and tentacles, she slithered up after me, her body undulating like a snake moving through grass.

I was almost there. A few more feet and— I lost my grip and slid. My chin grazed the rope on the way down; my hands, greasy with sweat, scrabbled as I vainly tried to slow my fall. Somehow I found a grip.

But now the Overlord was right behind me. I wasn't going to make it.

And then I saw it. Lodged in the ridge between the

window and the ceiling was a basketball—quite possibly stuck there as a result of one of my own wayward free throws, left forgotten over vacation.

As I stretched out an arm, my fingertips touched the ball. I had enough leverage to move it. The ball shot free. I juggled it in my palm, tensed in horror as it started to slide from my grip, and then somehow managed to control it in one hand.

The Overlord's gaping mouth rushed toward me, a shark rising from the deep.

There is a theory that an ordinary person can turn himself into an expert at anything with ten thousand hours of practice.

In basketball, I'd had two.

I had one shot.

Instinctively, I threw.

I knew as soon as it left my hand that I'd hit the target. The ball flew toward the Overlord's cavernous mouth, heading right down her throat.

But just when it looked like I'd scored the point of the century, another tentacle wriggled out of her mouth and, with a soft squelch, caught the basketball in its suckers.

The Overlord's laugh was deep and gloating. She wallowed in her imminent triumph. I gulped.

Suddenly, there was a crash and a tinkle from overhead. The Overlord and I looked up to see, through the falling shards of the shattering skylight, a masked figure swooping down, on full pigeon power.

Dark Flutter glided into the gym, coming to a stop in a perfect hover between me and the Overlord.

"Luke," she whispered. "Hold your breath."

Before I could ask why, Lara took a deep breath and filled her cheeks. Her hair stood up like needles, the ends glistening with some kind of liquid. And with a flick of her head she sprayed it into the Overlord's face.

Even from a distance, holding my breath, I could smell it. It was the worst thing that had ever gone up my nose.

The unfortunate Overlord took the full brunt of the attack. She inhaled the evil odor and began to gag. As she fought for breath she inadvertently sucked down the basketball.

It jammed in her terrible mouth like a hamster in a vacuum cleaner.

Slam dunk!

The combination of skunk attack and basketball in the cakehole gave her no chance. She began to choke. Arms and tentacles grasping for the obstruction in her throat, she lost her grip on the rope and fell to the floor with a crunching thud. She lay there between the volleyball lines and the tennis baseline, still and silent.

I turned to Lara. She was blushing furiously beneath

her mask, and wouldn't meet my gaze. "Zack couldn't make it in time. He sent me."

"Never mind him," I said. "I didn't know you could do *that*."

"So embarrassing," she muttered, snatching a bottle from her utility belt. "Dry shampoo," she explained. She looked around at me nervously as she pumped the contents onto her hair. "You don't think it's . . . weird and icky?"

"Well, yeah, obviously it is," I said, nodding enthusiastically. Her face fell. "But that doesn't take away from it being a totally awesome superpower."

"You really think so?" She perked up. "That's what I've been trying to talk to you about all this time. I knew if anyone would understand, it'd be you."

Well, that was a major relief. "So you don't want to be my girlfriend?"

"Uh, now who's being weird and icky? Luke, you're like a brother to me." She paused. "Or at least a first cousin."

There was a shout from below. It was Serge. I hadn't seen him come in. He stood as close to the stricken Overlord as he dared, pinching his nose. "She is still alive." He knelt down. "I think she is trying to speak."

Lara floated to the floor, and I climbed down to join them. Even with the basketball in her gullet, the Overlord managed to summon a few words. Her voice was a rasp. "Luke Parker of Earth, you may have defeated *me*, but there will be others. I am merely an overlord. Above me are executive overlords. And co-executive overlords. You have not seen the last of the sue-dunham. We will be back. After this break . . ."

One tentacle pried the whistle off her chest and stuck it in her ear. With the last breath from her strange alien physiology, she blew into it. An awful screeching filled the gym, and the Overlord was bathed in an intense white light. I threw up a hand to shield my eyes, and when I lowered it again, she had vanished. All that remained was her whistle. It fell to the floor with a clink.

THERE IS ANOTHER

"We can rebuild him. Better, stronger, faster," said Dad in a growly voice, and then he began to hum. *"Ner ner ner-ner . . ."* He noticed we were all staring at him. *"The Six Million Dollar Man?* No? Classic." He ruffled my hair. "Oh, you've got a treat in store, son. *Five* seasons."

It was a few weeks later, and we had just finished rebuilding the tree house. The workers—me, Dad, Grandpa Clive, Zack, Serge, and Lara—stood in the garden after a long, hard day, admiring our achievement. We'd started at first light (OK, after breakfast), and now the sun was low in the sky. Dad said it was like a scene from a film where Han Solo and a bunch of farmers build a barn in a single day. That sounded like the most boring Star Wars film ever.

"We should break a bottle of champagne over her," said Grandpa Clive.

"I thought that was for launching ships," I said.

"No, she's not a ship," said Dad. A wistful look came into his eye. "She's a castle in the air."

Although I had mourned its loss, I think in all honesty, Zack and I had outgrown the tree house. Dad was the one to suggest rebuilding it. I'd gotten the distinct feeling as the work progressed that he wanted it more than we did. Not that I was ungrateful. After all, S.C.A.R.F. needed new headquarters, and the tree house fit the bill, or would just as soon as I'd installed a few security measures. I wondered if we could also put in a toilet. That way, in the future, there'd be no danger of me missing Zorbon the Decider.

When everyone else had gone home, I sat alone in the tree house. I'd completed my homework for the evening, and now turned to the important job of setting down the S.C.A.R.F. code. Every secret superhero crime-fighting organization needed a set of guiding principles. I glanced down at the sheet of paper on my clipboard. It was blank. I tapped a Faber-Castell 9000 against my lip. Aha! I put pencil to paper and began to write.

>1. *Always follow orders, unless your superiors turn out to be a secret cult of evil cyborgs.*

There was a rustling at the door. Maybe it was Zorbon the Decider—we were due for another visit.

"Hello, son," said my dad.

"Oh."

"Were you expecting someone else?" He squeezed inside and took a seat beside me.

"Not really," I said, tucking the clipboard out of sight beneath my English workbook.

"I wanted you to be the first to know. Your mom and I have looked at the numbers. We're going to buy the comic store."

"You are?"

"I'll need you and your brother to help on weekends."

"That would be amazing!" My head was a whirl. "I have some fairly firm ideas about which comics we should stock, how we should display them, the launch party, obviously, and—" I grabbed the clipboard and tore off the top sheet. "I should make a list."

Dad smiled. "I think you should."

"Wake up," Zack's voice hissed in my ear.

I opened one eye. My Green Lantern alarm clock glowed on the bedside table. It was the middle of the night. I turned to my brother. He was wearing his Star Guy costume.

"What's happening?" I asked, sitting up with a start. "Is it another invasion?"

"Put this on and follow me," he said, flinging me a bathrobe. I pulled it around me, stuffed my feet into my slippers, and padded after him.

It had to be Zorbon the Decider! This would be his third visit to us now. I'd missed him the first two times, when he'd given superpowers to Zack and Lara. I tried not to get excited, but I couldn't help myself. Tonight was surely my turn. I had proved myself against the sue-dunham invaders. What higher reward could there be than to make me a superhero? But if not me, I really hoped it wouldn't be Serge. I wasn't sure that our friendship could bear it.

We slipped out the back door without waking Mom or Dad, and made our way across the yard. I glanced up into the night sky. The sue-dunham's fiery countdown still blazed overhead, permanently stuck at two seconds. No one had figured out a way to clean it up yet.

My heart beat faster as we reached the foot of the rope ladder. Zack shot to the top, and I hauled myself after him.

I had yet to add superhero lamps like the ones destroyed in the alien attack, so my eyes adjusted slowly to the darkness. I could make out the outline of two figures standing side by side. They were the same height. I recognized one as my brother, which meant that the other had to be . . .

"Zorbon?"

"Luke," said the figure.

"Zorbon?" I repeated.

"Luke," he said again. Something about his voice seemed uncomfortably familiar.

Zack threw open the wooden shutters on the new window. Light from the alien countdown made the inside of the tree house glow, and at last I could see who I was talking to.

He wore a mask and cape like Star Guy's. A superhero sigil blazed from his chest. Gloved hands lifted the mask.

He was me.

Not *like* me. Actually me. It was like looking into a freaky talking mirror. Apart from our height difference, he was my identical twin. Then I noticed that he wasn't taller than me after all. He hovered inches above the floor.

"You're . . . you're . . ." I stuttered.

"Yes," said the other Luke, placing his hands on his hips, puffing out his chest. "I am Stellar."

ACKNOWLEDGMENTS

One does not organize an alien invasion alone. Thanks to my editor, Kirsty "We come in peace" Stansfield, publisher Kate "Your weapons are useless" Wilson, Dom "Nuke 'em from orbit" Kingston, Fiona "No one can stop us now" Scoble, and the rest of the hive mind at Nosy Crow; thanks again to illustrator Laura "Destroy all humans" Anderson and designer Nicola "It's a trap!" Theobald for the stealth technology cover to fool the earthlings. I am grateful as ever for the invaluable strategic advice of Agent "My mother ship is bigger than yours" Stan. And finally, a world-flattening laser destructor blast of thanks to the woman whose existence ensures I always know where to direct the aliens when they say, "Take me to your leader," my wife, Natasha.

DAVID SOLOMONS has been writing screenplays for many years. *My Gym Teacher Is an Alien Overlord* is his second book for children. His first, *My Brother Is a Superhero,* won the 2016 Waterstones Children's Book Prize. He was born in Glasgow, Scotland, and lives in Dorset, England, with his wife, novelist Natasha Solomons, and their son, Luke, and daughter, Lara.

READ MORE ABOUT LUKE, STAR GUY, AND THE IMPORTANCE OF ALWAYS CARRYING YOUR DEADPOOL BACKPACK IN . . .

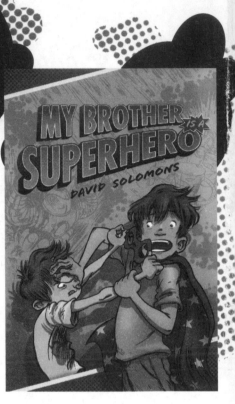

When Luke Parker's boring, teacher's pet brother Zack gets turned into a superhero, Luke can't believe the unfairness of it all. But when Zack—aka Star Guy—gets into super-size trouble, it's up to Luke and his intrepid neighbor Lara to rescue his big brother and, with a little luck, help him save the world.

★ "A non-stop action-packed, laugh-out-loud winner of a story."   —*School Library Journal*, starred review

"As genuinely open-hearted as the genre that inspired it."
                —*Kirkus Reviews*

"Solomons demonstrates that he's equally at home with high-octane comic-book action and more ordinary topics like the pain of being overshadowed by an older sibling, superpowered or otherwise."   —*Publishers Weekly*